RAISING SAMARA

RAISING SAMARA

STARLETTE CARVALHO

PARTRIDGE
A Penguin Random House Company

ISBN: Hardcover   978-1-4828-5182-3
               Softcover   978-1-4828-5181-6
               eBook   978-1-4828-5178-6

Print information available on the last page.

To order additional copies of this book, contact
Partridge India
000 800 10062 62
orders.india@partridgepublishing.com

www.partridgepublishing.com/india

CONTENTS

CHAPTER 1

Lawrence Barreto

Finding refuge in an abandoned house, I gathered a dense handful of twigs and dried leaves and built a small pyramid. Reaching for the matchbox, I brought light into the darkness. Reserving my exploration of the house to just six feet of survival space, I used an old T-shirt to dust the floor to lay my body down to rest.

I grew up hearing a lot of scary ghost stories. Goa is filled with tales of paranormal activity. I even saw a ghost cow once.

It all happened four years ago, when I was just sixteen, as I rode my bicycle back home. I took the usual route from my buddy Carl's house to mine in the early evening. Roads were deserted as early as seven thirty.

A small bridge connected the villages, and as I neared it, a whole stretch of streetlights went off, one after the other. As if this wasn't bad enough, the headlights of my bike flickered off, too. I looked ahead, but saw no one on the street. I threw some holy words at the headlights and the bulbs, which I had only just installed. I slapped it hard in a fit of anger, for leaving me in the lurch—pitch darkness surrounding me—while still in motion it felt offended and came on immediately. I looked straight ahead, and BOOM! A white cow's face appeared in front of me. To avoid hitting the cow, I veered to the left and skidded off the tar road and onto the unpaved portion mostly made of native red gravel. I looked to see if I'd upset the cow and if she planned to charge me, but, to my horror, I saw no cow around. I picked up my bicycle, took the shortcut, and sped for home. Friends who heard the story laughed at me. My mother said the cow was an angel who came between the devil and me by blocking my path and diverting my direction. Folklore of Goa.

Still, the incident shook me and made me fearful of darkness for years.

But tonight, I had no fear. I knew I was being watched, not by one, but by two guardian angels. My parents had left for their heavenly abode this past New Year's Eve.

Lying on my back, I studied the sky full of stars through a missing tile on the roof, trying to connect the twinkling dots into an outline of the faces I missed here on Earth.

My dazed and sedated senses took me to another dimension of happier times. My eyes felt heavy from lack of sleep. Within just a few seconds, I nodded off.

The sounds of muffled voices awakened me from my slumber.

I shouldn't have built the fire. No doubt, seeing the light and smoke in a rundown house had brought panic in the village.

The villagers of yore would avoid dealing with the unknown and rather pray to the gods for forgiveness and thanksgiving the minute they suspected wandering spirits, but we, the new folk, were too curious for our own good. Just as James Stephens put it, "Curiosity will conquer fear even more than bravery will." So there they were, "Ghostbusters," barricading all the exits of this forsaken mansion. They armed themselves with, *coita*, slingshots, knives, and cane sticks.

"Who is in there? Come out, you scoundrel!" shouted the head of the assemblage.

Shouts of agreement from the villagers followed.

I was doomed. There was no way out of this. I needed divine intervention. A hope that they would care to listen before reacting.

I knelt down and, eyes shut, recited the Memorare.

The villagers began walking towards the door. Unsure of where the courage came from, I voluntarily pushed open the door, and with both hands up in the air, I walked out. My eyes squinted at the sharp rays of sunlight that engulfed me.

The swarm of people stopped marching forward and were now scanning me for any abnormalities. *Was I human or was I a ghost?* They studied me carefully.

I began to plead with them, when one of the members of the crowd hurled a brick towards me. I flinched, and flinging my arms up to protect my head, ready for the impact. "God, save me," I blurted out.

A hand pushed me to the left, and I fell to the ground, the brick missing me by an inch. A Savior He did send.

"Why is no one giving him a chance to justify himself? Look at him. Does he look like he could hurt a fly?" asked a youthful, yet authoritative voice. I opened my eyes to see a five-foot-ten-inch figure wearing denim twill tape cargo shorts with a creased olive green t-shirt

"Stand up," he said, looking down at me. "What are you doing here?" he questioned, demanding a sensible reply.

"I needed a place to rest for one night," I answered, helping myself up.

"Who else is with you in there?" He glanced back behind my shoulder, toward the front door, which stood gaping open.

"No one," I replied immediately.

"See? This is no monster. Let us go back to doing important things," he said, addressing the crowd. "And you. Come with me," he commanded me to follow him.

Without questioning his judgment, the congregated crowd followed him out of the gate as if he were a pied piper leading the way.

Whoever he was, I knew that instant, that he was my Savior, and I was willing to follow him.

"Lawrence Barreto," he said, introducing himself.

"Daniel," I replied submissively. "Daniel Carvalho."

Those were the only words shared on our silent two-hundred-metre walk down a well-trodden road leading us away from the sparsely populated area and into the densely populated neighbourhood.

One of his comrades pushed open a huge iron gate and led us toward a fair-sized villa built of red sandstone.

"*Gharamai*," called Lawrence. This was a common nickname for grandmothers in Goa. "We have a visitor; please bring some *poi* and *kalchi kodi* for us all," he requested in a loud shout.

There was no response from or sight of the *Gharamai* he called. I began looking around at the inside of the mansion. The seating furniture was ancient, made of wood and thick plastic strings pulled tightly across them. There were two living rooms that, together, had the dimensions of a tennis court.

From between the curtains appeared an old woman, about five foot three, with wrinkled skin and wise old eyes, who slowly shuffled her way towards the dinner table.

She smiled at me and walked right back in the direction she came from.

"She cannot talk," muttered Lawrence. That explained the unresponsiveness to the call from her grandson. "But she has excellent hearing, like a cat." He grinned as he sat down at the old dining table and motioned for me to do the same. I slid into an old chair, glancing uneasily at the others who crowded into the room.

"What brings you to our village?" Lawrence asked, his sharp eyes missing nothing as he studied me.

He maintained a strict, no-nonsense demeanor. I wasn't sure whether I should make up a story or just be honest. Running away from home out of sheer boredom didn't seem the right answer at the moment. I could make up a sob story worthy of the hundreds of Hollywood and Bollywood movies that I had watched over the years. But then again, I would need ten more lies to cover that one. I didn't want to make the effort. Lying is so much tougher than telling the truth.

Lawrence appeared to be an insightful man, and one with a solid perception of intellectual concepts, good foresight, and an understanding of life beyond what most youngsters his age have. Why would he have a village listening to him otherwise? A young *Sarpanch*. Isn't that rare.

In minutes, I found myself pouring out my soul to him.

I loved my parents and they loved me. I thought I'd had the perfect life with them. They loved me unconditionally, and life with them had been like a wish list always granted. When they died, and I moved in with my grandmother, everything changed.

She had requested that I live with her at Divas Village, a decision I grew to regret.

Divas Village was a place where the mobile network poles, erected by the telecommunication team, were broken down by the few existing villagers who believed that it affected the fetuses of pregnant women. Pig latrines, the chirping of crickets as early as six thirty, the no loud music zone, a strict military-like regime, the constant reminder of my parents' untimely deaths, all contributed to sucking the life out of me.

A quarterback star of my college, I felt reduced to nothing. I did not want to be a part of that ghost town.

I escaped the place of confinement with a farewell note on the table under the altar.

With this, I ended the recitation of my saga.

They were deeply stirred by my story.

"Would she file a police complaint?" Lawrence inquired doubtfully.

"No, she wouldn't," I asserted.

"What did you write on the farewell note?" Lawrence wanted to make sure that it wouldn't be a police issue.

"Here, take a look. I took a picture of the letter I wrote." I showed him my phone.

It read:

> Dear Nana,
>
> I am leaving. I hate this place. I hate the confinement and the reminders of the loss of my parents. So I have to leave. I am sorry. But I must go. I will be safe. I will call you soon. I love you.
>
> Your grandson,
> Daniel

"Did you call her?" Lawrence asked after reading the letter.

"Not yet," I answered.

"Give her a call. Tell her that you are safe and that you will keep in touch." He nodded at me. "Make yourself at home until you find a place of your own. There's a guest room at the end of the hall. You can stay there."

I glanced at the other men in the room. None spoke out against Lawrence, and they all stared quietly. Lawrence motioned to them. "This is Victor, Nigel, and Michael." I nodded back at them.

Victor and Michael looked like twins. With identical features and dimples on each of their left cheeks, both men were of short stature. Nigel was around five foot six and frowned at me.

"Go ahead, make the call. We'll give you some privacy." They stepped out of the room as I dialed Nana. She answered on the second ring. She was happy that I had called and that I was safe, but upset that I had left in the first place. I told her I was at a friend's place far off and planned to pick up a job and stay here for a while.

I also gave her the hope that I would see her soon. After the call, I stepped out of the room to update Lawrence on how the conversation had gone.

There was no one around, so I began exploring the house.

A spiral staircase led upstairs from the hall to the upper floors, where three out of the six rooms were located. Two of the three rooms were well-kept and inviting. The third room bore a huge Godrej lock on the door and a message that read, "Caution: Once in, there is no way out." I heard footsteps downstairs and ran to the bottom and into the guest room that had been offered to me. The cozy bed invited me to relax my body, and soon, I slept like the dead.

Dusk came the following day, and along with it the team of four marched in and went straight upstairs, into the room with the message of caution on it. I had spent the whole day besieged by boredom, so I rushed behind them, hoping for the chance to chitchat, but was stopped at the door.

"Daniel, didn't you read the message on the door?" Nigel snapped, angry.

Lawrence intervened. "Why don't you watch some television downstairs? We'll see you in a bit."

Curious about what could be behind the door, but in no mood to fight about it, I retreated. I made my way to the living room and glued myself in front of the boob tube.

Garamai was watching one of those *saas bahu* serials. I couldn't tell the difference between any of them, but it reminded me of my mother and her contest with my father over TV time, especially when the T20 matches were on.

"What are your plans, dude?" a voice behind me questioned.

It was Lawrence. Was that a response to my inquisitiveness or was he wanting to know how long I would be a pile on?

"I will start to look for jobs tomorrow morning, as well as paying guest options in the city," I replied.

"I didn't mean to offend you. I am sure you would like to justify your choice to run away."

Lawrence had a genuine, concerned look on his face.

I had dropped out of engineering college suddenly, and didn't have a clue on the know-how of the corporate culture. Where should I start? At twenty, my only achievement to date had been football. I thought of my last game. That game ended 3-2, and I had scored one goal, made the other, and got Man of the Match award. My coach noticed my potential and suggested my name for the Elite Football

League of India, which was only recently founded. Of course, all this came before the catastrophe of my parents' deaths. After they died, I didn't much want to play football anymore. I didn't much want to do anything. But some time had passed, and now, I had begun to feel differently.

"Football; yes, I would like to join a club," I said, thrilled at admitting the truth of what I wanted to do.

"Daniel, my friend, you should start your search tomorrow. Follow your passion," he said. Then, he paused, as if reconsidering. "Just let me give you a piece of advice, since I have been there, done that. We all would love to follow our passion, but something we need to think about is whether our passion would endure amidst competition, bribery, selection process-rigging? So keep in mind that you might need to consider an alternate means of livelihood."

That night, I reflected on what Lawrence said. He wasn't crushing my passion, exactly. He was warning me of what to expect and advising me to always have a back-up plan. There was no easy route to becoming a footballer. To join the club of the elite involved a lot more than just being a good player.

Over the next few weeks and months, I played charity matches for recognition. But, no matter how well I played, it didn't seem anyone noticed.

I considered seeking Lawrence's advice on what I should do next. I was beginning to feel desperate.

One evening, I was in the kitchen, looking for a snack, when he and Nigel walked in. Nigel has a perpetual frown as a default on his face. He has no social skills whatsoever. Neither was he the friendly, talking kind.

I sensed right from the beginning that Nigel was not happy about Lawrence's decision to let me stay, while Victor and Michael were affectionate and caring towards me.

It made sense to wait for him to leave, which I did, before talking to Lawrence.

Close to bedtime, Lawrence settled in to watch TV. I took a seat next to him and said, "Lawrence, I heard you are an entrepreneur."

"Where did you hear that?" He appeared suspicious for a moment, as if I'd stumbled onto a secret he didn't want me to know.

"Your grandmother told me."

"She spoke to you?" he asked, looking skeptical.

"Not exactly. I have been spending time with her and have begun to understand her gestures," I said. "Would you have a job for me? In your ... business?"

Before Lawrence could respond, Nigel came out of nowhere. He barged into the conversation and very hurriedly said, "It's Michael. We need to go. He is so yacked out at Uncle Ben's Bar, he picked a fight with a cop."

No other words were exchanged. Lawrence stalked toward his Maruti Omni parked in the garage, and Nigel and I followed.

We drove off to the city police station. I waited with Nigel in the car, until Lawrence returned about fifteen minutes later, supporting Michael, who could barely walk. Nigel ran to help him. We stopped a few metres away, and entered an empty row-house Lawrence had the key for.

Placing Michael on the sofa, Lawrence walked into the kitchen and sat at the dining table, running his hand through his hair.

"Why would he do this?" he asked Nigel in a stern voice.

"I don't know. I'm just glad the bartender gave me a heads-up. His meeting went sour, and he ended up sniffing the stuff and whacking the daylights out of the client," Nigel replied sourly. Lawrence frowned, disapproving.

"Daniel, you want to join my business, do you?" Lawrence asked quite unexpectedly as he leaned back against his chair. "Can you be discreet?"

It had dawned on me that Lawrence and the team were part of a shadow world. That Lawrence, along with being a pied piper, was a highly influential person who dealt with illegal stuff.

Still, I nodded.

"Good," Lawrence said. "So the both of you stay with Michael tonight. I have to get back home," he said and got up to leave.

Nigel followed him to the door. They had a whispered argument that didn't reach my ear. Nigel frowned at me. It appeared he was objecting to something. Probably me.

That night, the secret that had been so carefully safeguarded, unfolded itself. By this time, I didn't need to be told Lawrence was a drug peddler. Michael, working for him, had been trying to sell drugs at the bar. What else would he have snorted? It only made sense, Lawrence supplied drugs to the tourists and the clubs in the north of Goa.

"You better not do anything stupid," Nigel warned me, eyeing me fiercely. "Lawrence has a soft spot for you, but I don't."

"Why do you say a soft spot?"

Nigel shrugged one indifferent shoulder. "He lost his parents, too."

I hadn't realized that. "Why? Drugs?" Nigel looked surprised.

"No, they didn't do drugs. Why do you say that?"

"I mean, I know that's what you do. It has to be drugs," I added. "I'm not blind."

Nigel weighed his doubt as he decided what to reveal to me about Lawrence or what they did. I could see suspicion in his face.

"They died one after the other. One, a heart attack and the other, a stroke. After Lawrence's parents died, his grandmother was diagnosed with breast cancer. He needed to make money quickly to get her the medication she needed, and once you are in it, it's difficult to get out," Nigel concluded.

I didn't judge what he did for a living. I knew he wasn't a bad man. I saw how much kindness he bestowed on the poor and needy. He'd turned his parents' house into a home for the elderly. His grandmother worked as the manager.

Lawrence was a selfless person, always giving, always standing up for what he thought was right. Someone who was respected.

He was a victim of circumstances that could force any youth to mature very fast, and a traumatic enough life could burn the teen right out of you.

"He has invited you to join us. It's at your discretion," Nigel said, and then walked towards the living room to check on Michael. The way he said it made me think he wanted me to say no. I wondered if he was jealous of the attention I got from Lawrence.

The next morning, I woke up to the smell of coffee and the sound of jumbled voices.

I followed the aroma of the coffee that led me to the living room, where Michael was being bombarded for his negligence.

Lawrence pushed a fresh cup of coffee in my direction. I picked it up and went over to the balcony.

I had decided to take the leap of faith. Fate had turned everything in my life upside down, and dumped me into a world where the only certainty at this point was Lawrence.

I was already greatly indebted to Lawrence for rescuing me from stone-pelting and providing me free shelter. After losing my parents, subconsciously, I had been on a constant search for a mentor, my life coach. A search for that one person I can turn to for an answer to all of my questions. Lawrence seemed to fit the profile. He was a good listener plus someone who withstood all the odds life threw at him and turned every rejection into acceptance.

I needed money to survive. I could make some cash out of this to pay him back. The question was: Could I do it? Did I have the nerve? If by some freak accident, I got arrested for selling pot, would I have the courage to bite the bullet and go to jail? Lawrence was influential, though, and knew every cop of every *taluka*, so I hoped that didn't happen. I was in safe hands. I guess.

It was amazing how much can go through our mind in just a second. As I approached Lawrence, drinking coffee in the living room, I knew I was ready to take the dive into the abyss.

CHAPTER 2

Anne and John

For the next two months, Lawrence invited me to join him on several delivery runs to pothead clients, an introduction to the products, services, target audience, existing clientele, and existing distributors in the market. He gave me extensive training and guidelines on survival skills, staying unnoticed, always spending in cash, keeping an alert and sharp mind and tricks to memorizing phone numbers, quantities prescription, as well as time and date of delivery. Physical records were a big no-no. He told me to write nothing down. Do not use contract cell phone plans. Use multiple pre-paid contact numbers and change phone cards frequently. Don't engage in conversations with strangers making any enquiry. Always just sit back and listen, suss the situation out, keep quiet, and let things unfold. Verify any new contacts.

What I noticed was that there were many people like me in the field already. Competition was steep, considering the loss of employment the great recession brought. It appeared that resorting to grass distribution was the next best alternative to make ends meet.

Selling pot was tricky, but also kept many people employed. To be successful, I found, the most important trait to use was common sense.

Love and relationships were not good for our business. I found out quickly that the drug business caused collateral damage. It didn't take long for love to turn to hate or greed or vengeance. Friends took liberties in long credit periods, which sometimes turned into bad debts.

The most offensive business required each of us to own a pistol. Shooting was forbidden, but we needed them to intimidate, or, as a blunt-force option. Lawrence gave me a pistol with no bullets.

"Pistol-whip the guy, don't shoot him." Lawrence would reiterate this *mantra* to the team. Requesting us to keep our tempers in check and never panic or get into unnecessary brawls with crack heads, which would lead to letting the cat out of the bag on what we were up to.

We were also required to look our best at all times. People had an image of what a stereotypical drug dealer would look like. Police watched for the stoned, or heavily tattooed. We were to look like fine, upstanding, regular citizens, the last person you would ever suspect. Lawrence said it was the best way to hide in plain sight.

Inventory was split amongst Lawrence, Nigel, and me. Nigel would not use dope, aside from one toke from every batch to ensure the quality of the stuff. Yes, quality control exists in this business, and Nigel was the quality control manager.

Since Victor and Michael had families who were not aware of their occupation, they could not keep any stock with them, lest their secret be discovered.

Neither Victor nor Michael was in this to build an empire. This was a temporary solution, just to help them make enough money to settle with their extended families in Swindon, UK.

"When are you going to move out?" Lawrence asked me suddenly.

All of a sudden, I felt like a guest who takes *minha casa é a sua casa* too seriously. I was embarrassed by Lawrence's public questioning.

The question left me frozen. I didn't have an immediate response in my head. The others in the room looked at me as if there was blood running down my forehead. "I-I-I don't know yet. I could rent a room somewhere," came my feeble, stuttering response. *Rent a room? How would I pay for it?* And why was Lawrence suddenly in a hurry to get me out? Questions pacing in my head, fingers crossed, I waited for Lawrence's response.

A phone ringing brought a pause to the conversation, while Lawrence was speaking to one of his clients.

"Dude. Listen. It's not like Lawrence wants you out of the house," Victor said, reading the awkwardness of the situation.

"You know you can stay with us anytime you like," he continued. "It's just that we follow strict ground rules. We cannot live in close proximity of each other or meet daily. It will look suspicious."

So that explained why Lawrence was pushing me to leave.

He finished with his call and turned and looked straight at me.

Perhaps hoping that the length of time between me answering the question and him finishing the call would have been sufficient enough for me to find a place to shift into, immediately. But I was still at a loss.

"I have a place for you," Lawrence said. "My row house at St. Anthony's colony. Shift in there." It wasn't what I expected. Nevertheless, I was elated by the offer.

Nigel's reaction was priceless. The perpetual frown that adorned his face was now joined by the pink color of rage.

"Guys," Lawrence continued, looking around to the others, "this is the last month of the season. Let's make some big bucks," he said, to which the team nodded and began to give each other high fives. Everyone, of course, but Nigel, who continued to pout.

I was excited to move into my new home. St. Anthony's colony.

I loved it. It was centrally located, with a panoramic view. Lawrence had furnished the spacious two-bedroom villa with modern furniture.

I moved in with only my luggage. The faithful, flashy American Tourister hiking backpack, which contained pretty much all I owned, two pairs of casuals and one pair of formal clothing, three pairs of underwear and three pairs of socks, a simple set of toiletries, one pair of casual shoes and one formal.

Lucky for me, the house was fully furnished. *Someday, I thought to myself, someday, I will own a house as beautiful as this.*

The colony had a great mix of people. This time, though, it wasn't free lodging; I would pay Lawrence rent. This was extra motivation for me to meet my targets. I met some of my neighbours, but decided to keep a bit of distance. The less they knew about what I did for a living, the better. And the best way to make sure they didn't know was to keep to myself.

Some of my neighbours seemed fine with *not* knowing me. For instance, the beautiful lady who lived next door. On any given day, to get her to even say "hi" back was like pulling teeth. I didn't even know her name. She'd always frown at me and rush away, hurrying her little boy away from me as if whatever I had might be contagious. I didn't know why she didn't like me, but she clearly didn't.

Sometimes, I wondered if she suspected I worked for Lawrence, *and* what that meant. If she did, she didn't say, but she clearly wanted nothing to do with me.

Not long after my move, Lawrence introduced me to his business connections.

I researched the products I was selling just like any enthused salesman. Slowly, clients began to value my encyclopedic knowledge of the products and chose to deal with only me. My youthfulness and charm ensured more referrals and repeat business.

Thus began my journey into the wonderful world of opioids.

I was honestly pro-alcohol and not weed. So selling the stuff I didn't believe in but that generates loads of *moolah* needed research. A drink always warmed the buyers' feelings. What I liked best about alcohol was that you can have a few drinks without tripping or being drunk.

Unfortunately for me, I had a lot of client meetings and began drinking too much and too often. I tried smoking the stuff we sell, too. The thing with weed was, you cannot get a *little* stoned. You have to get all the way stoned. Sex, too, is such a dampener when stoned.

My youth and money seemed to be a seminal catalyst for increased female fan following. Women don't date low-earning men. They didn't seem to care about how we earn it, only how we spent it. Floor them with expensive bags and shoes and you up your probability of having them in bed with you. I found more than my share of luck in this department.

It was a good month. I came in just under the top salesman. Nigel retained his number-one position. I chose to keep it that way for a couple of months, hoping that he'd warm up to me.

The off-season slowed down business. Yet, despite the decline, I loved the monsoons in Goa. The pitter-patter of the raindrops was music to my ears. The smell from the land seemed like incense to me.

Tourists didn't know what they were missing. Frog hunting, the rivers overflowing, the hills and sidewalks covered with greenery, the sweet smell of mud … ah … Goa was at its best during the monsoons.

Local bars never shut up shop, come wind or storm, and the Goan cashew feni is the cheapest alcoholic beverage available. You can get a bottle of cashew feni for Rs. 75. What scotch was to Scotland, champagne to France, tequila to Mexico, vodka to Russia, feni is to Goa.

My favorite hangout was Uncle Ben's Bar. I was there one night with Victor, Nigel, Michael, and Lawrence; we sat at a table and ordered a round of cashew feni, while I concentrated on rolling a joint.

Lawrence broke my concentration and asked me to continue the rolling on a toilet seat, lest it attract unwanted attention.

The news of Michael Jackson's death was doing the rounds on TV. The bartender was playing ode to the greatest entertainer of all time—MJ.

Victor stood up and entertained us with some of MJ's signature dance moves, owning Uncle Ben's limited dance floor. He emulated the moonwalk with panache. Lowering the heel of his left foot and raising the heel of his right, he kept gliding backwards across the floor, amidst a lot of hooting and clapping. He reached out for his glass on the table and drank it all in one gulp. His thirst was not quenched so easily, apparently, as he then drank from all our glasses. "Hey, take a drag off this spliff, and go ahead, dance like no one's watching." Lawrence offered the joint. *Puff, puff, puff.* Victor inhaled, and broke the circle- passing rule. It was always puff, puff, pass.

On the floor again, this time, he wanted to show off the gravity-defying lean move. His toe gave way, and to the floor he went. Victor was wasted, and someone had to take him home.

The rain stopped, and I decided I had better get a move on before the downpour began again. Umbrellas had a certain way of disappearing. Once, I had a collection of umbrellas and rainwear, but now I had none.

I was so inebriated that I could barely see the path ahead of me. It was a good thing that public intoxication was not considered an offence here. Stumbling and taking smaller steps than usual, I could see home in the distance. Just like a marathon runner taking his last lap, I started increasing my pace.

Home was about four metres away. I was drunk, maybe not staggering drunk, but drunk enough to impair my judgment. Unexpectedly, a young child slipped off the steep pathway of his house, along with his bicycle, and landed on the road with a thud. It was a little late for him to be out, I thought, wondering why he was riding at night. It all seemed fine until I could hear the squeal of tires and flash of headlights, which came from not too far. Without looking around to judge the distance of whatever the tires carried, I knew it was heading for the child on the road, who looked helpless struggling to pick himself from beneath the bicycle. I leapt to him, picked the bicycle up, along with the boy, and landed in a well-kept garden alongside the road. I could hear screaming and shouting. I fainted. Or passed out.

In any case, much, much later, I was awakened by a shrill voice piercing my ears, like nails on a chalkboard.

"No! Stop it! Clear the mess right now!"

The voice spoke with too many exclamations. *An exclamation-mark abuser,* I thought. Trying hard to inspect the surroundings with my eyes squinting and blinking rapidly, I couldn't tell where I was. My body felt sore and my mind, numb. I could barely release any words from my mouth. Yet, I needed to know where I was. I'd passed out in the dark, and woken in the light, so I assumed I'd slept the night.

Blurry-eyed, I noticed a small figure running into the room. The figure looked at me and then swiftly started searching for something. Getting hold of a hardcover book that probably weighed more than him, he threw it on the floor with a thud. My once-squinty, blurry vision saw clarity instantaneously. My mouth still agape, I glanced around me. Was I in a mental asylum? I lay on a well-kept bed with white sheets on it. Very limited furniture adorned the room. My neck swiveled in a sudden display of flexibility, desperately seeking an exit option. I surveyed my surroundings. It was a cozy room, and the walls were painted light green. A huge closet with Disney posters stuck on it faced me. Nearby, a study table sat stacked high with books, including, *The Complete Guide to Tailoring.*

The wall had a write-and-erase weekly planner, which had a to-do list that was practically full all week through. The woman with the shrill voice was clearly very organized.

"Oh! Hi! Good morning," the shrill voice boomed. "How are you feeling, a … a … aah?"

Now that she was in front on me, I recognized her. The beautiful MILF who lived next door. Didn't recognize her son though. "How did I get here?" I asked.

"You don't remember, do you? You must be famished. Let's talk over breakfast. See you at the dining table in ten," she said and stepped out of the room. I felt relieved that my house was right next door.

I eyed the Disney posters on the door. Aladdin, Pocahontas, The Lion King.

"Breakfast is served," she called out. Goan *pav* with sunny side up eggs and bacon. We took our seats at a four seater dining table made of teakwood.

I started on breakfast and quickly devoured it, like a street urchin who had not been served a meal for a while. Looking up from my cleaned-to-the-crumb plate, I felt embarrassed. They hadn't even started eating. The young boy was looking at his plate as if wondering what to start eating first, the egg or the bacon. It was obvious with the shifting of the fork from the egg to the bacon and back. Eeny, meeny, miny, moe.

My pretty neighbour was poking at her breakfast. I took the liberty of looking at her.

She did not have a ring on her finger, and there was no hint of a male presence in the house.

"This is my son, John, and I am Anne," she introduced herself. "Daniel Carvalho, right?" she asked gently.

She knew my full name. I had not introduced myself using my full name to a single soul in the colony.

"Apologies in advance, but the name came from the driver's license in your wallet, which is lying on the study table," she said, pointing toward it. *How did she get it out of my back pocket? Did she undress me last night?* I looked at my clothes to see if they were any different from what I had worn the day before. They weren't.

"Oh. Thank you for breakfast," I said, while picking up the plate to drop it in the kitchen sink.

"Don't worry with that." Anne stood up to stop me from entering the kitchen.

"So what happened? I remember having a fall. I am sorry if I caused you any embarrassment."

"Embarrassment? No! Daniel …" She bit her lip, tears springing to her eyes. "Daniel, I want to thank you. You saved my son's life," she said, sobbing now. "He … wasn't supposed to be out, but sometimes he sneaks out of his room, and …"

I sat down at the dining table, forcing myself to recollect the events that had unfolded the previous evening. I did have an unstructured flashback, though I was not sure whether to discuss it or leave it be.

Anne volunteered to narrate the incident.

She had thought her son was safely tucked in bed, but John had sneaked out to ride his bicycle. The veranda slope was steep, and unfortunately, due to the rains, there was moss growing everywhere. The bicycle, with John aboard, slipped and landed on the road.

Then I remembered: the kid on the bicycle.

"You picked him up and …" She choked back tears.

"Now, I remember," I said, stopping her.

She surprised me with a hug. I hugged her back. I must admit, nothing says it quite like a hug.

"I am grateful to you," she murmured, pledging her loyalty to repay me for saving the life of her son.

The image I had of Anne had transformed in a jiffy. From a woman with narcissistic personality disorder into a warm, loving human being.

I wasn't sure whether I should enquire into her personal affairs. She wore no ring, but was she married? What did she do for a living? I decided to leave it for another day.

Waving goodbye and feeling on top of the world, I headed home. I had saved a life.

CHAPTER 3

The Neighbours

It is always a great feeling to return to the warm and cozy comfort of your own bed. As I was about to hit the deep sleep stage, the loud ringing of the phone woke me up.

"Hello?" I croaked.

It was Lawrence. "Hi, buddy. Come on over."

I knew it would be a bad idea to tell him no. Normally, Lawrence would call when the sun dipped lower in the sky, so this must be an emergency.

"On my way," I said.

I was still enveloped in the grogginess of sleep, and it was minutes before I found myself rising from beneath the comfort of the quilt to the edge of the bed.

I was the last to arrive at Uncle Ben's Bar. Our meeting place. Uncle Ben had been a friend of Lawrence's dad. Lawrence pumped in cash whenever necessary into this bar and restaurant. A family-owned simple set up. Round plastic tables and chairs, with red-and-white checkered tablecloths, dotted the dining room. A ten-square-metre bar area served the finest liquor in the whole of north Goa. Lawrence made sure imported liquor was stocked at all times. The bartender, the son of the late Uncle Ben, loved to experiment with cocktails. His cocktails had exotic names, like Fiery Dance, Komodo, Sinker, Dandy.

I took my seat.

Lawrence treated us to the Indian scotch-style whiskey Royal Stag.

"What's the occasion, dude?" Victor asked cheerfully, pouring a big shot and drinking it straight up.

"Thirsty, Vicky?" the sound of his enormous gulp forced me to enquire.

"Yes," he said, pouring another shot.

"Back to your question, Victor. Yes! We have every reason to celebrate this afternoon. I have just collaborated with a weed farmer," Lawrence disclosed with great joy. The last quarter, the supplies had been surprisingly limited, so this was very good news, indeed. Some personal issues had hindered contribution from one of our main suppliers.

"Now we need not worry of the supplies. Let's toast to that," he said, and raised his glass. We did the same. "Oh, and we need to double up our sales," he said with his glass still raised, truly 'Boss' style. With regular and dependable supplies, we could now go after the bigger fish in the sea.

There was a brief moment of silence, and I took advantage. I started talking before we all slipped too far into a state of oblivion. With great pride in my heroic deed,

I started to tell them the story of how I had saved a life the previous evening.

The three of them looked at me with an expression of admiration, or so I thought. A few seconds later, Michael, raising an eyebrow, said, "Anne, huh? And you slept at her place last night?" He grinned at me, oblivious to the good deed. "She is a divorcée. You know that, right?" He elbowed me, his meaning clear. I chose not to reply.

Lawrence took my side, and gave Michael the shut-your-trap look. The conversation was over. It wasn't heading in the right direction.

Victor always seemed to be in a state of disconnectedness, even when he was around people.

He was writing something on the napkin from the table. Nigel pulled the napkin from under Victor's palm and started reading out loud:

I had a dog whose name was Snowy,
He was loved and was such a homey,
With him there was never a day that went by lonely,
I miss him and his memories I will cherish ever so dearly.
I will never ever own a pet again,
For my heart, forever, with you will remain.
This void no one can fill
Not even your girlfriend, Jill.
No one to lick the many cans of beers
Oh! Snowy! The pain, of a thousand spears.

Shocked, Michael asked Victor, "You had a dog we never heard of?"

Victor shrugged, obviously feeling burdened by the loss of his dog. Nigel returned his napkin and changed the topic.

"Victor, you should really come to the party tonight. It's going to be so much fun, and there's going to be pretty girls galore," Nigel told him.

"She is a strong, wayward, stalwart, and ambitious woman," Lawrence said suddenly, and I realized he meant Anne. "Anne stitches the best wedding gowns in the whole of Goa, and that while also juggling housework and a dumb child."

"Dumb child? Why would you be so judgmental of a three-year-old kiddo?" I questioned.

"Judgmental? I didn't mean dumb as in stupid, I meant dumb as in voiceless," he clarified.

"Yeah, unfortunately, his mute button got stuck," Nigel said and laughed unkindly.

"What is with your juvenile sense of humor, Nigel?" Lawrence scolded.

On my way home, my thoughts fled to the things we take for granted. The air that we breathe, the food we get to eat, the house we call home. So many things we take for granted—things others pray for.

As I was almost home, Anne stepped out to say hello. She noticed I had my wobbly boots on. She elected to walk a few steps with me until I was at the door.

"Karaoke tonight. My place at nine," she offered. "I know you are flying high with the fairies right now, but please, I want you to come. I will come over to wake you up." She seemed to know that if I hit the sack, I wouldn't wake up until sometime tomorrow.

"All right," I said. It sounded fun.

At nine sharp, my doorbell rang. I opened it to find Anne on my porch. I could see traces of makeup, making her look even more luminous than usual.

"I came over to wake you up, but you seem fresh as morning dew," she said and chuckled. Her once-screechy voice now sounded sugary.

"I had a friend over, so I didn't sleep," I lied. There was something magnetic about her. As she studied me, I realized she was someone I would like to spend time with and get to know better. *Okay! I like her,* I admitted to myself.

As she turned to lead the way, it gave me a good chance to check her out. Her hair was midnight-black, and it plunged down past her shoulders. She wore clothes in an unconventional way. She had a sculpted figure that was twine-thin. Who would ever imagine that her body had been through the major process of pregnancy, labor, and childbirth? It didn't appear so.

She turned to look at me and smiled in awareness, knowing that she was being noticed. Her set of dazzling, angel-white teeth gleamed. I loved her nebulous, big brown eyes, which had a sparkle with a *joie de vivre*. They were like two precious jewels that glittered under the night sky.

Without a shadow of doubt, she was a man-magnet. I could see what Michael meant when he'd gone on about her at dinner.

We walked through her door, which was left ajar, and I saw a group already gathered in her house.

With shock, I realized I recognized all the faces, even if I didn't know all of their names. It was our neighbourhood.

All of St. Anthony's colony members were seated in her spacious living room.

Until then, these neighbours had treated me like an outsider. I didn't blame them. Lawrence asked me to keep a low profile and stay away from nosy neighbours. I was following his instructions, so I mostly kept to myself.

I went over to greet Jacob and Dasy D'souza. Not because I was fond of them, but was drawn to the rocking chair near them. It looked comfortable and inviting.

Jacob and Dasy D'souza's villa sits across the street from my house. A part of their house had been converted into a grocery store that stocked everyday necessities.

"Greetings, Mrs D'souza," I went up to her and said. Mr D'souza had to step outside to attend to a phone call.

Besides Anne, these two were the only neighbours I shared any verbal communication with. The others, I knew by sight only.

"Hi, son. It is so nice to see you here," she replied cheerfully.

She always referred to everyone she knew as "son", "daughter", "darling", "sweets", or "sweetheart". I suspected it was easier to do this than remember people's names.

I took a seat next to her and looked around the room. It was decorated with paper lanterns and streamers hanging loosely from the walls.

There was a "Happy Birthday" banner hung up, along with a sign that read: My Boy Turns Three. It was John's birthday party! As I looked at the table in the corner, overflowing with wrapped presents, I realized I was the only guest in the room without a gift.

My eyes searched for Anne. She was busy setting the table with the Superman-themed Thermocol disposable crockery. I waited.

She came around with a tray, serving black plum cake.

"Anne, this is embarrassing. Why didn't you tell me it was his birthday?" I questioned, feeling awkward.

"Chill, Daniel. You are here. That's what's important. You don't need to bring a gift! You've already done so much for us," she said loftily, while moving over to Mrs D'souza with the tray.

"I should have brought John something!"

"You gave him 'today', Daniel. You saved his life. What greater gift would you be able to give on his birthday?" she said with quiet empathy.

"Daniel, we heard what you did. We are very proud of you, son," echoed Mrs D'souza.

John came running up to give me a tight hug. He spoke with hand gestures that I did not understand. But, as his lips moved silently, I realized he was saying thank you. I suddenly felt overwhelmed—I'd never expected so much warmth and gratitude. I'd just reacted in the moment to save him. I hadn't thought about it. I hadn't even planned it. He held my hand and guided me towards the center table, where a Superman cake was ready to be cut. He continued holding my hand through the cake cutting.

Shortly after, Mrs D'souza began to tell me about the other guests at the party. "We have three doctors in the house. That is Brian and Joyce Noronha," she said, pointing to a couple in the corner. "Brian is a general practitioner, while Joyce a gynecologist. The irony is that they are childless.

Then you have Brenda Fernandes. She is a pediatrician. She is currently working with Bumble Bee Nursery as their primary care pediatrician."

"What about her?" I asked about the older lady in a wheelchair, who was carefully eating a piece of cake.

"Mrs Braganza is paralyzed. The lady next to her is her nanny. Her son pays ten thousand rupees to the nanny for the up-keep of the house and the old lady." Mrs D'Souza nodded to the woman talking to Mrs Braganza. "That one there is Samantha Rodrigues. She is very nosy. Stay away from her. She always has to put in her two cents worth. She lost her husband last year. She didn't wear black clothes for more than a day. She does volunteer work at the orphanage down the road."

Just then, Brian, one of the doctors, stepped up and introduced himself.

"Hiya, Danny. I am Brian. I am sure Mrs D'souza has told you all about everyone in this room by now," he teased.

"Yes, she did. Very kind of her," I replied.

"So, what's up?" Brian found it a struggle to make conversation, one could tell. He had a marine haircut and serious eyes. His thinly plucked eyebrows were framed on a pleasant face. He obviously paid a lot of attention to self-grooming.

"The ceiling, with a very pretty crystal chandelier," I responded playfully.

"You certainly do have a funny bone," Joyce Noronha said as she joined us. "What do you do for a living, Daniel?" she asked.

"I am a salesman. I sell prescription drugs to pharmaceuticals," I lied, but it was as close to the truth as I could get.

"Really! What kind of drugs?" Her curiosity increased.

"Hi, guys!" Thank God. Anne interrupted the conversation.

"So, Daniel. Did you meet the doctors?"

"I certainly did," I said, grabbing John and trying to sneak out of the conversation.

"Thanks for making it, you two. They're as busy as bumblebees," Anne said.

"Not as busy as you are," Brian replied.

"Season time must be tough on you," Joyce continued.

"Yeah, right. It's not like climbing Mount Kilimanjaro, Joyce. I sew for a living," Anne said, flashing a grin.

"How would I know, sweetheart? Never even climbed a sand dune before," Joyce said and laughed.

Pouring herself a drink, Anne raised her cup. "Let this cup of wine always overflow," she said to the gathered neighbours.

I noticed from the corner of my eye that Anne poured herself a large shot of tequila. She drained the glass in one gulp. *It had been a long week for her,* I thought, remembering the agenda she had scribbled on the wall calendar.

As we came to the closure of the celebration, the guests started returning home.

For me, the night had just begun. I wanted to stay on.

"Anne, I heard you stitch the finest bridal wear in town. Must be tough." I was looking for a conversation starter.

"Yeah, I dress young ladies for the most special day of their entire existence. The irony is, I hate that day. I hate weddings. I hate marriages," she said with a sad grimace and poured another tequila shot and downed it.

Anne was alone. She was hurt. Her eyes filled up with tears. I offered her a tissue to soak the tears from her eyes so that they wouldn't run down her face and ruin her beautiful makeup. I didn't want her to cry. I don't know how to handle emotions.

"Was he abusive? He fell out of love? Did he cheat on you?" I asked all the questions that I thought were the most common reasons one hears on a marriage turning sour.

She shook her head to each one.

"No, he was a loving man. A loving man who was afraid of responsibility. He could not handle being a father to a mute child. I had to be around John ninety percent of the time. We argued over John all the time. He wanted John gone. Gone away to a special needs centre to be looked after by nannies. How could I do this? He is my son! John isn't an easy child. He has his tantrums and needs attention all day," she cried.

"I really loved Agnelo. He was all I had. One day, I spoke to him about seeking help from a counselor. He agreed. But the next day, he was gone. Gone forever. To date, he has not contacted us," she said, clearly still grieving.

I wanted to hug her, but didn't know if I should. I reached out and touched her shoulder. She sniffled back her tears. I didn't know what to do, so I changed the subject, hoping to focus on something other than sadness.

"So, does he read lips?" I enquired into John's condition.

"Yes, he does," she replied, as she swiped at her eyes. "He is going to a mute-program in Pense. They put heavy emphasis on lip-reading and using sign language. I have to attend the classes with him as well, to understand and learn sign language so that I can help him communicate. His educational and social experiences are different from the rest of us," Anne explained.

"Isn't there any operation that can install a voicebox?" I asked, not sure if I used the right words to describe the process.

"It is some sort of genetic disorder. My great grandfather suffered from it. The doc said if I was aware of the genetic predisposition I should have gone in for an adoption instead," she said.

"Anyway, what this experience has taught me, is that you do not need a voice to communicate. You just need people who want to communicate with you, and the rest will work out. I am his voice now."

I held her hand and gave it a light squeeze. I wanted to tell her that she was doing much better without Agnelo and that a man running away from his responsibility was a worthless excuse for a man. I stopped the words from flowing out of my mouth. I looked at my reflection on the glass table. I had no room to talk. I was a worthless excuse for a man. Look at where my life was heading. I might have saved her son, but I was still selling drugs. And I surely had not taken anything in my life seriously up until now.

We all carry emotional baggage to varying degrees—painful childhood memories, grief over the loss of a loved one, the devastation of a marriage or relationship break-up. Or, in my case, the death of my parents, which I still hadn't really truly processed.

"Anne, you know you are quite a lady, right? Independent, loved by all …"

"Don't go overboard with flattery," she remarked, cutting me off.

"Let's sing one more song to end the night, shall we?" I said, changing the topic.

We sang Bill Withers' "Lean on me".

Chapter 4

The Kiss

A stereo vibration, stamping feet, and sporadic clapping woke me up in the wee hours of Wednesday morning. *What the hell!* I thought. I shuffled around on my bed in an attempt to drift back into sleep, but the Latin music captured my attention enough to wake me up entirely. Cuban Pete. *Oh Boy!* Twenty-one-year-old Cameron Diaz in the movie *Mask* was on everybody's wish list. Women included. Many fantasies were brought to life with her grand entrance, red dress, and red lipstick.

I looked at my bedside clock and saw it was eight in the morning. I searched for my phone, wondering if Victor had changed the ring tone again. The last time I was at a client meeting and my phone rang, it had been the, '*I like to move it, move it*' tune. I was embarrassed. Victor changed the ring tone purposely with the intention of shaming me.

This time it wasn't him, though. And the heavy vibration was shaking the miniature bottles off my wooden shelves.

If a wake-up call was earlier than 11.00 am for those who toiled all night, Lawrence would say, "Whoever blesses his neighbour with a loud voice, rising early in the morning, will be counted as cursing" and defended it, as it was a phrase he picked from the Bible.

I stepped outside, and my ears directed me to the arena. It was Anne's house. What on earth was she up to?

I rushed ahead, to understand what joy she was getting by waking the neighbourhood up, mid-week. Of course, I knew most of the neighbourhood was probably awake already. 'Snoozers are losers!' Anne would often whine about my sleeping pattern. I was one of the few neighbours who worked odd hours, though, so the regular cock-a-doodle-doo morning alarm did not apply to me.

As I walked through the door, my jaw dropped to the floor as my eyes opened wide to the sight of a room full of women of all age groups lost in dance and music. Sweat glistened on their foreheads.

"Carry on," Anne instructed them. Some of them were unhappy with the intrusion.

"Hi." Anne smiled at me. "Is it something important?" she whispered. "Can it wait?"

"No!" It took me about five seconds to remember my reason for being there before I spoke.

"Why so early? Can't you be doing this later in the day?" I pulled a very unpleasant face for a moment and then grunted loudly. It was obvious I was not happy to be woken up so early.

41

"Not exactly early for the world outside your house," she reminded me calmly, not feeling at all guilty for waking me up.

"The rest of the world is already up and at work, you know."

"Whatever! What is this new act, anyway? Some Goan Broadway show coming soon, or is it in preparation for the carnival?" I asked mockingly, now wide awake and trying to fight back my giggle.

"Shh. I will explain later. Half an hour more. Breakfast is in the kitchen if you would like to stay." She directed me to the kitchen and went back to dancing.

They were following a Zumba fitness DVD.

With the kitchen door left slightly ajar, I watched them dance. Anne had cleared the furniture from her living room to make space. I spotted John. He had joined them, right at the center. Like the anther on a sunflower.

Whilst picking at my breakfast of cheese and bread, I watched Anne. She was dressed in black leggings and fuchsia pink spaghetti top with florescent green Reebok shoes. She looked like candy. My eyes were fixated on her dance moves. Totally surprised by the sensual dancing and sexual waves that emanated from her, I pictured us in a club, grinding.

Snapping of fingers in front of my face broke the daydream.

"Daydreaming with your eyes wide open?" Anne asked, while serving John breakfast.

Yes. You and me. Grinding in a club. But I didn't say that.

I controlled those thoughts and forbade them from reaching my lips, lest she think I was a douchebag.

I tackled the question with a lie. "I was sleeping with my eyes open," I claimed, wanting her to feel a sense of guilt.

I went straight to the point, curious to know how and why she had a battalion of women in her house so early in the morning, dancing with so much energy.

"Nothing much, *yaar*. Women, tired of the regular gym routine. They find it very boring. In fact, gym has become more of a meeting place now, just like coffee. Less working out and more gossip," she said.

"So you brought the workout home," I summarized.

"Yes. Kind of. Evette, this friend of mine, discussed the idea with me. She is Zumba certified. We decided to charge a small fee. Kill two birds with one stone" she winked. "Make some money and add some swing to these ageing bones".

Women make it big as entrepreneurs. They think outside the box.

Anne was a multifaceted individual; she knew how to juggle being a full-time mother, a fashion designer, a tailor, and now, another feather to her hat, a Zumba Fitness Trainer. She knew how to live life queen size. I couldn't help but admire her. She had her priorities straight. Her son, John, was at top of the list. She was doing a great job raising her son. She was one smart, highly productive woman.

After that, I'm not sorry to say, her house became my one-stop pantry. I probably shouldn't have eaten so much of her food, but it was so good and she offered it so freely, that I couldn't help it.

Every Wednesday, she would conduct her Zumba classes, and she encouraged me to be a part of it. I eventually became a fixture in this class, unable to help but ogle the gorgeous women trying to sweat it out. Classes would go on for an hour, but I would find a way to sneak out for a *puff, puff, puff.* She completely detested this and wanted me to change my lifestyle.

She became a part of my every waking and sleeping moment, one of my few good habits.

Every night when I staggered home drunk, she would chaperone me to my doorstep and tuck me into bed. Our bond was unexplainable. Yes, it started with me saving John, but it grew into something more than that. I had some karmic connection with her that produced a natural high. She was eight years older than me. But then again, I had never dated age-appropriately. I've always dated older women. There was just something that attracted me to them. They seemed more mature, more intelligent, and thus more attractive to me.

"You have got to do something about the smell of weed, which is no longer confined to just your house," Anne warned me one night whilst tucking me into bed. "Before you get busted by nosy Samantha, you know." She pulled the sheets over me and bid me goodnight.

She was right. I didn't want the neighbours thinking I smoked weed, nor did any drugs. I didn't want them to know what I really did for a living. St. Anthony's Colony was now like family to me. Changing the paint of the walls on my house is easily done, but I cannot repaint a tarnished image. I decided I needed a stock of perfumed incense sticks, candles, and some air fresheners.

Anne wasn't oblivious to my profession. She knew exactly what I did and never needed an explanation.

She was well-connected. She had her sources who gave her information, but she did not judge me based on the information.

Ours was the easiest relationship I had been in for over a decade. Based on the principle, "You ask no questions, I tell no lies!"

I gave her a key to my apartment. She was reluctant to keep it. She wasn't sure what I was implying. I told her I didn't want her to knock and wait. I would rather have her just walk in whenever she felt like it. Just as a matter of convenience.

But then again, I had never given the key to my house to anyone before. Subconsciously, I felt an unshakeable trust and connection with her.

"Are you sure you want me to keep the spare key?" she confirmed again, clearly understanding the need for privacy in my life. "I mean, you have guests …"

She meant the parade of strange women in and out of my bedroom. None of them stayed long. It didn't matter to me if they knew Anne had a key.

Anne had bumped into Sandra, who tiptoed out of my house at dawn a few days ago. The unfortunate bit was, she knew Sandra. It's a small world. Sandra was a bridesmaid at her friend Kyra's wedding, and a family friend.

She remained tight-lipped about it, never even mentioning it to me. It was Sandra who informed me that Anne, a snarky smile on her face, had asked her, "How is Uncle Frances?"

Uncle Frances was Sandra's dad.

"Yes, babe. You now have access to my private life," I asserted. "So, now, if you want to chase off all the girls, you can do so with a key."

"I don't care who you sleep with! And I am not your babe!" she said rigidly.

I nodded. "Okay."

She looked at the key, considering its implications.

"I'm not giving you a key to my house," she said.

"Not yet," I said, and she gave me a playful shove.

She smiled and left.

***

It was the end of another successful month. I had now beat Nigel at sales three months in a row, and I was the new reigning champ. I had decided to stop treating the man with kid gloves. He didn't respect me, whether I let him keep his number one spot, or took it from him. I decided I was tired of holding back and I'd rather earn cash than save Nigel's ego.

To celebrate, I treated the team to drink and dinner at the *Kiki Lounge*. One of the new high-end clubs that attracted wealthy clientele.

"Nice work, Daniel," Lawrence said, raising his glass and guzzling it in one gulp. "Let's get *shammmered*, guys," he slurred, already having a few put away. "It's Danny Boy's treat!" He ordered another round of tequila.

Victor and Michael came around to give me a congratulatory hug. Nigel stood six feet away and watched. He didn't look happy. How long could I keep trying to please him? I had done everything I could think of to earn his respect and friendship. It was his fault he didn't accept it.

It's my success. My celebration. If he wants to sulk all evening, so be it!

Around two that morning, Lawrence dropped me home.

Anne's living room lights were on. I wondered what she was doing up so late. Not Zumba dancing, I supposed.

I stood at her front door, staring at it for a few seconds, then turned around and walked over to my house. She probably accidentally left them on after a rigorous Zumba session, I decided.

Her door opened while I was struggling to put the key into the keyhole of my door.

Brian and Joyce Noronha walked out of it and kissed her goodbye.

"Hi, Anne," I called out.

"Oh, hi!" she said. She came over to help me with the key.

"You had a late night, huh? I wasn't invited?" I said with a sad face on.

She threw her head back and laughed. "Since when did you become a drama Queen? King? Whatever…" She skipped ahead of me into the bedroom, where she straightened out the covers. She picked up the ash tray and an empty beer bottle, while giving me that disappointed nod.

She walked past me to dump the litter into the kitchen bin. She smelled like her familiar scent of fruity freshness, and I breathed it into my nostrils and felt an arousal. Anne was … beautiful. We really should get together. I wanted her, yet in my alcohol-fogged mind, I didn't know if she wanted me. Should I try?

I followed her like *Cheeka* the pug, who aired on the "You & I" advertising campaign of Hutchison Telecommunication Service.

"The bed isn't calling you, yet?" she asked. "What's on your mind, Daniel? Want to talk about it?" She paused, looking at me expectantly. I'd never found her more deliciously attractive than in that moment.

"It's you I have on my mind," I said, putting a steady arm around her waist and pulling her close to me.

I bent over and covered her mouth with mine. Her lips tasted like strawberry syrup.

Drawing a deep, shocked breath, she pulled herself free.

"Daniel!" she protested, refusing to look at me. In my alcoholic haze, I didn't know what to make of it. For a second, I thought she had kissed me back, but now, seeing her flustered, I realized she was shaken and annoyed. Maybe she didn't want me at all. My heart sank.

She tucked me into bed and turned to leave. I held her hand and stopped her.

"Anne, I'm sorry. I … didn't mean to … Do you have to go? Why don't we stay up and chat?" I desperately tried to think of something to say. She didn't leave. She stayed on. "Ever fallen in love?" I asked, still holding the palm of her hand.

"What is love to you? Nothing!" she quickly uttered. I guess she was referring to the women who walked in and out of my door on a regular basis.

"Anne, I know what you are thinking. But they are not looking for love in me, nor I in them," I said, bringing her fleeting thoughts to a halt. What was I saying to her? Would I want her to fall in love with me? Would I want more from her? "You know women. They can't seem to make up their minds," I continued, trying to shake off the ice-cold Casanova image she was building of me.

"FYI, I recently read an article on the Web on sexual energy cords. Out of the energies available at our disposal, sexual energy is the most powerful. It intertwines your aural energy with the other person's aural energy. So you really need to pay attention to whom you share that sexual energy with, lest you take on all their negative energy," she explained.

"Google! A blessing and a curse!" I remarked. "Why must you think so much? Just go with the flow!" I tried to convince her to live for the moment and not worry about what tomorrow would bring. But then again, I was wrong. She was a stalwart believer of love and marriage, while I was a lovestruck Romeo.

Knowing she must put an end to this scary tête-à-tête, she gathered herself, and leaping to her feet, said abruptly, "I have to go, Daniel."

I sank into my sheets with myriads of thoughts racing through my head. I hoped I hadn't scarred our friendship.

Sometime later, my growling stomach woke me up. The birds were up, singing their waking song. I went over to Anne's to grab a bite and also to apologize for my misbehaviour the night before. She welcomed me in her usual way, as if nothing had happened the night before. I was grateful I hadn't ruined things. Maybe I'd just pretend I was too drunk to remember what I had done. Yet, as I watched her move around the kitchen, I wondered if that was what I really wanted. She whipped up a plateful of bacon and scrambled eggs for me.

John watched me eat. The boy loved me. Maybe he needed a father figure. Luckily, we shared a common passion: football. After breakfast, I showed him some tackle tricks in the yard. He hopped around like a kangaroo with the ball, and his wavy hair made him look über cute.

Now, he dribbled the ball right past me. I turned to look at him and saw Anne joining the game.

"Anne, did I screw up last night?" I asked.

"Screw what?" she asked naughtily.

"Us," I replied.

She laughed and shook her head. "No way," she assured me.

"So are we good?" I asked again, wanting to make sure.

"All is well," she said and nodded.

Thank heavens for a friend like Anne. There is no melodrama; it is always cut and dried. I felt relief, I decided, as jumping into a personal relationship with her probably wasn't wise. Anne deserved someone who was serious, and I didn't know if I was capable of being that person.

She was a wonderful neighbour and friend. I wanted her, but not bad enough to ruin what we had. After Mum and Dad, there was Lawrence. I shared a dependent relationship with them. With Anne, it was more.

It was strange, given that, with any other woman, if it wasn't purely physical, I was never interested.

CHAPTER 5

Mr Navekar

I woke up early the next morning. Too early, and to the sound of heavy knocking on my door.

I knew it wasn't Anne, because she had the key. Why did everyone in the neighbourhood want me up so early?

I glanced out and saw a man who looked a lot like Mr Navekar, an anti-narcotics cell officer. I knew him on sight because Lawrence had pointed him out once on the street. Mr Anand Navekar, a stout, five-foot-four-inch man, had a bushy moustache, a beer belly hanging out of his khaki shirt, and smelt like deep-fried sardines. He was deployed at the corner of Calangute Beach, a place where Nigel pushed most of his business.

According to Lawrence, Nigel and Navekar were buddies, and the fact that he was knocking on my door this early told me Nigel had put him up to it.

Nigel quite wittingly befriended Mr Navekar. Fighting weight issues, low self-confidence and living hand to mouth were a few of the stumbling blocks in his life. Nigel capitalized on them. Cash gifts were presented for Diwali and Christmas. There was a lot of improvement with his self-esteem thereon. Mr Navekar, in turn, would blame the Israelites, Russians, and Nigerians for pushing drugs in Calangute or send him after Lawrence's competition. Never had he ratted out one of Lawrence's boys, but I supposed there was always a first time.

Nigel must hate me even more than I had imagined.

The knocking continued, like a woodpecker tapping on a tree. Thank God for the entrance view from my bedroom window.

The thing was, I never answered my door early in the morning, mostly because I switched the bell off and because no one usually knocked that hard. Besides, Anne or Mrs D'souza would always take a message for me if it was urgent. This morning wasn't any different, and besides, I had company. I glanced over at my bed and saw a naked girl I'd picked up from the night before. I couldn't very well open the door with her lying beneath my sheets. She must have been a sound sleeper, I decided, as the knocking didn't rouse her at all.

Mr Navekar continued with his thunderous knocking and calling out my name until it reached Anne's ears. She stepped out, and walked in through the main gate of my house.

"Yes, Officer," she said. "Can I help you?" She sensed trouble and put on her best smile.

"Have you seen Daniel this morning?" he asked curtly. He clearly had his investigative hat on.

Anne was not good at thinking on her feet, but she managed an excuse. "I sent him to the pharmacy to get medicine for my son. Can I take a message for him?"

A crowd started to gather. Any event on the street attracts a horde. A bystander effect. It has been studied that single bystanders are more likely to help than a group. The more bystanders there are, the less your chances of getting any help. People take cues from others, and if no one else moved to act, they wouldn't either. The police uniform always drew curiosity.

Mrs Braganza prayed at the cemented cross. On seeing the officer, she wheeled herself over to become a part of the gathering.

Mrs D'souza, too, came to speak with the officer and provide support to Anne if required.

"What is it, Officer?" Mrs D'souza asked as she approached.

"Oh, it's police business. We are just working on a lead," he said to her.

"Daniel is like my son," Mrs D'souza said, taking pity on me, as the neighbours had done since Anne took me under her wing. She had the whole neighbourhood convinced I was a poor orphan, just trying to get by. "The nicest boy in the locality. I am sure whatever brought you here is one big mistake," she said, trying to butter up the police officer. He didn't seem to be buying it, appearing more interested in creating some ridiculous charade.

The officer frowned.

"I hope he is everything you think he is, ladies. I'll be back," he said, in a very Arnold Schwarzenegger from Terminator way. He climbed into his Jeep, and with one more look at my door, drove off.

I was glad to see that Anne and the neighbours handled the situation perfectly for me. I felt lucky to have such good friends.

I slipped back in bed to suffer through one of my worst hangovers. My one-night stand grumbled and rolled over as I slipped back in beside her. I had already forgotten her name, and if I fell back to sleep, I might very well wake and find her gone, which was fine by me.

But that was not going to happen.

Several minutes later, Anne opened my door and rushed into the bedroom. She found me naked, with a girl in my bed. She threw the sheet over me to cover my body.

I whined. My head was pounding so bad I couldn't concentrate on hearing anybody. My throbbing head was in no mood.

"Daniel! Wake up," she said and gave me a hard slap across my face.

The stinging pain made my eyes pop open. My headache was gone, but my cheek ached.

"What the hell, Anne? I am awake! You gone mad?" I screamed. She didn't say a word but kept switching her eyes back and forth from the bed to me.

By now, I had forgotten that I had company. "Hey, wake up," I said, nudging the lady in my bed. She groaned.

"Why? Let me sleep a little longer." What *was* her name?

Charmaine? No. Brenda? Nope. She was this Hindu girl I bumped into in the billiards bar down the road. *Sonal! Yes, that's it.*

Anne picked up her clothes and threw them at her face and asked her to leave. She sat up groggily and stared at Anne.

Anne didn't stop there. She pulled the sheets and exposed Sonal's naked body. She didn't care much if that exposed me as well.

Jumping off the bed, Sonal charged Anne like an angry bull. Anne stood still like a pillar of rock. She stopped Sonal with one firm hand. Then, without any exchange of verbal words or physical abuse, she indicated strongly for her to leave the house.

Sonal wasn't left with much of a choice. She looked at me for help. I didn't want to get involved, and instead, walked into the bathroom, unable to decide whose side I should be on. Both were right to me.

"Daniel, Inspector Navekar was here!" Anne said, walking straight into the unlocked bathroom. "This is no time to mess around with … the likes of her."

"I know. I saw him." I scratched my head. "Thanks for saving me."

"Why were they here, Daniel?"

I shook my head. "I don't know, but I'm going to find out." I had my theory that Nigel was behind it, but I didn't have any proof.

"If the neighbours get a whiff, they will collectively want you thrown out of this society! Samantha will complain to the cops," she was mumbling nervously.

After pulling on some clothes, I called Lawrence immediately and had him speak to Anne. She explained to him what had happened.

She then passed the phone to me.

"Don't worry, *baba*. I think I know what happened. He is Nigel's best buddy." Lawrence clearly suspected foul play.

After the call, I gave Anne a hug. She shrugged it off.

Lawrence called again. This time to let me know that Nigel would no longer be working with us. I figured that Nigel's jealousy got the better of him. It was too bad he couldn't just get past it. Now, he'd be out of work.

Apparently, Nigel had grown jealous of my success, and he paid the officer to bust me, only to shake my ground a bit, which is what brought Mr Navekar to my door.

Jealousy is like Alzheimer's disease, as it has three stages: mild, moderate, and severe. The first two stages can be fought off by some self-control, counseling, and self-reasoning, but at its severe stage there is no help.

I thought about this as I sat in my empty apartment. Anne had gone home, and now the sky was full of tumultuous dark clouds. I stepped out to catch up with the rest of the gang. We would have a structural change in the organization with Nigel gone.

Through my window, I noticed Anne pacing around in her garden, confused and tense. Something had upset her, and it wasn't just the officer at my door. She still looked angry.

Briskly walking to and fro on her twelve-foot veranda, she also looked a little nervous.

Was she upset about the girl in my bed? Especially after I had kissed her a fortnight ago? I thought she might be.

I decided to go over. "Need a hug?" I asked, approaching her.

"What?" her expression changed from tense to one of surprise. She didn't budge.

"Okay! I need one!" I wrapped my arms around her before she could protest and hugged her tight.

After all, Mr Navekar's visit had now become an albatross around my neck. I hated the fact that he had put the neighbourhood in a frenzy over a personal issue. Regardless of Lawrence's conviction, I was disconsolate.

I was worried to make eye contact with Mrs D'souza, as I knew she would think an explanation was in order, and I had no idea what to say.

I kissed Anne's forehead. I could feel her tension, and now her comfort. I stepped back and was glad to see her smile.

"I am heading to catch up with Lawrence. See you in a bit," I said, feeling that I had handled the situation well. I started walking away.

She followed me out and stopped me by throwing her arms out, creating a barrier.

"Hold up," she said. Her face tensed again.

"Anne. Is this about the …?" I asked, figuring we needed to clear the air.

Anne dismissed the thought in my head. "No," she blurted, a little too loudly. "I don't care who you sleep with. I only hope you are playing it safe. Goa is on top of the states with AIDS-affected patients." She glared at me. I wondered if it was truly just my health and well-being that bothered her.

"Yeah, Anne. I do not sleep with prostitutes. I sleep with friends and acquaintances," I said, assuring her I play it safe by knowing the people, but I was only half-joking. She didn't like the joke.

She laughed it off. "You should still *use protection*," she murmured.

Her fumbling fingers lent me a paper and pen. She was holding an envelope.

"What is this?" I asked quizzically, wondering if she was going to give me lessons on playing it safe.

"Oh! This is a pop quiz for you. Your award is in the envelope," she said with some uneasiness and a pretend smile. "I will ask the questions, and you would just need to write down your answers. So, are you ready?"

"Can this wait?" I was in a hurry to meet with the gang.

"Please. This won't take more than ten minutes. I promise," she said with a low-browed, saddened mien.

"Yes, quiz master," I said with a wink, indulging her. For some reason, this seemed important, so I figured I'd better do it.

"First question: What would you need to get your energy boost first thing when you wake up? Would it be coffee, tea, horlicks, or alcohol?"

Alcohol, I wrote. Of course, I need a drink to begin my day. With the first question itself, I knew where this was heading.

"If you were to propose to a girl, what would you do? Think of a creative line, buy her a diamond ring, or drink up a couple of shots and blurt it out?"

I wrote, *Blurt it out after three shots of vodka.*

"Have you woken up sober once in the last one year?"

No. Not that I remember.

"Do you wake up sometimes not remembering what happened before you could hit the bed?"

"Is that a trick question?" I asked before jotting down the answer.

A couple of times, yes.

"Oh, come on, Anne." I grew impatient with the questions. "How much more and why?"

She stopped and evaluated my sheet.

"Do I get the envelope now?" I asked.

She handed me the envelope and turned away. Was she shy, scared? Ugh, women! They are so complicated.

The envelope header stated, "Come and have some fun in sobriety!"

It was an invite to an Alcoholics Anonymous group.

It was only after we talked more, that I realized her nerves in confronting me came from the reaction of her husband, who walked away when the idea of counseling was suggested and chose to stash their six years of marriage without a conversation on the subject.

"You want me to try this out?" I asked out of concern for her feelings and to ease her tension.

"Only if you want to," she said.

"I can try sobriety my way, too," I said, assuring her that I could get off alcohol easily. After all, I didn't really think I had a problem.

"I am sure you can, but this would give you an opportunity to get together with people, too." She clearly felt strongly about this. She wasn't letting it go.

"Okay! I will go," I said, figuring it was no big deal. Besides, I didn't want to argue with Anne, and how hard could it be?

Then, I rushed out to catch up with the guys over Nigel's dismissal. I thought about what Anne had said, and the quiz she gave me, and figured after one meeting, they'd see I don't have a problem. What was one meeting? I'd go, and then they'd tell me I shouldn't even be there. That thought made me feel better.

But I had questions too. Why did she care? Did she like me? Did she think that drinking made me vulnerable to one-night stands? What if I did go to AA? Would she like me more then?

Chapter 6

AA and Karen

The villa could not be missed. It stood out, a vibrant blue-and-white structure, with a covered porch held fast by Cluster columns. Large stained-glass windows faced the street, and a well-kept garden surrounded the house, and its Goa-Portuguese architecture likely cost a fortune.

The villa, named Derrame Sua Alma in Portuguese, meant "pour your soul". My heart rate sped up, and nervousness gripped me as I walked up to the house. I hated attachments for this reason. They brought in a whole lot of obligations. I did not understand the need for me to go to this association, conference, or whatever it was called. I didn't want to meet people, talk to strangers, and overload my brain with nonsense. I wanted to run away. If Lawrence ever found out about this little stunt I was trying to pull off to please my neighbour, he'd never let me forget it. I'd be the butt of his and everyone else's jokes, and with Nigel gone, and because of the way it happened, I was not sure he would appreciate any more emotional drama.

I considered for a second making up a little white lie and not going. But then I thought about lying to Anne, and my stomach twisted into a knot. I didn't want to lie to her or disappoint her, I realized, so there was no getting out of it—I had to go.

I was confident I didn't have a problem, and yet, with Anne so adamant, it made me doubt myself. *I guess the meeting will help me find out,* I thought.

Anne cleverly booked the meeting in the North of Goa, knowing that I would not go if it was anywhere in our neighbourhood. What if others thought like Anne? What if I did know someone here?

Climbing up the seven-step staircase of interlocking pavers made of red concrete, still dubious about the whole idea, I turned my back toward the front door.

It swung open.

"You must be Daniel," said a woman in her mid-forties, wearing a dark blue suit, a nicely tucked-in white formal satin shirt, and a pair of branded glasses that polished off her professional look. She smiled warmly.

"I am Lorraine Alberto."

"I-I-I," I stuttered, as thoughts raced through my head, endlessly tripping up my words.

"Daniel, come on in, and please, try to relax. No anaconda is going to swallow you in here," she said, trying to put me at ease. It worked.

Disarmed by her kindness, I swallowed my misgivings and allowed her to lead the way. She took me down a long hallway to a living room with an anticipated circular seating arrangement of folding wooden chairs. There was no escaping visibility in a circular arrangement like this one, unlike in a classroom, where you could take the last bench and indulge in origami or even catch a nap. People already occupied most of the chairs. I was late. There was a bulldog clipped whiteboard lying on a chair, which I assumed was the chair of the speaker. The only two empty chairs were right next to it.

Movies played a pivotal role in my imagination, drawing a picture of what an AA meeting would look like. I looked around and expected a room filled with eager, restless, drunk kids; however, there was a good mix of individuals, both men and women, young and old, who all looked sober and serious. Was I at the right place?

Nobody seemed to be interacting with each other. Eyes followed the host wherever she went.

Deeming it wise, and for the sake of amusement, Mrs Alberto asked me if I preferred a nickname.

"Danny is good with me." I waved reluctantly to the seated group. Only one or two of them waved back.

"Welcome, Danny," they all said in unison. I took a seat and relentlessly embraced the burning flame inside my mind. I took a quick glance at my watch, hoping to be out of there in thirty minutes flat.

Mrs Alberto emphasized the fact to the group that Alcoholics Anonymous, was a social gathering centre, where fun and laughter were the key features. It was a fellowship of men and women who come together to share their experiences and help each other achieve sobriety.

There was no such thing as dos and don'ts, and the cultural rules that were applied in the other associations would not apply here.

"No stereotypical introductions are accepted," Mrs Alberto announced, pouring herself a cup of coffee and suggesting for us to grab one. None took the coffee invite. We definitely wanted one, we were just too shy to step up to it.

"And please save me from, 'Hi, my name is Johnny Joker and I am an alcoholic,'" she said, her big brown eyes wide open and glancing across each one of us. I knew right away this was like no AA meeting I'd ever heard or seen before. They were all centered on rigid rules and twelve steps, or so I seemed to recall.

A soft foam ball was used as the introduction icebreaker, and when Mrs Alberto tossed the ball, the recipient would introduce himself or herself any way they would like, but she asked that the person try sharing some interesting facts, memories, embarrassing moments, or family dramas, all of which were welcomed.

Mrs Alberto threw the ball toward a frail, yet handsome young lad who seemed ready, almost like a catcher located behind home plate in a baseball game, making me think her choice had been premeditated, and the two were in collusion.

He made no introduction, just started his life story.

In his desire for a well-sculpted, lean and chiseled muscular body, Edgar had decided to take performance-enhancing drugs and Human Growth Hormone (HGH). These drugs were sold at local gyms without prescription and without the knowledge of the authorities. Over the last couple of months, he found the drugs had side effects: he had severe joint pain and numbness of the skin. The general practitioner referred him to an endocrinologist after Edgar confessed using drugs like HGH. The endocrinologist told him the tragic news. He had leukemia. The high levels of HGH stimulated the growth of the cancerous cells. Currently undergoing chemotherapy, and soon, a stem cell transplant, Edgar had turned to alcohol to ease his mental and physical pain, though he knew that was not right, either. He had come to the group to help him get sorted out.

I looked at him and thought that explained the frail frame, the constant sipping of water, the couvre-chef neatly tied over the bald head, and his shortness of breath.

Edgar tossed the ball over to Nico, a fair-skinned youth in his mid-twenties with droopy eyes.

"I started drinking when I was ten years old," Nico said, clearing his throat. "The descent into alcoholism was but natural in any Goan household. We inherit the trait from our parents, our peers. The house parties welcomed a lot of drinking and dancing, and I would simply pick unattended drinks and down them and loved the feeling. At school, I drank the local liquor feni or urrak."

Nico also said he stole money from his parents to fund his alcohol habits. He was thrown out of college eventually for lack of attendance. When he couldn't afford a drink, he would scout the local pubs and went minesweeping; he landed up in rehabilitation centers, where he masterminded an escape with three other fugitives from rehab. His parents spoke to Mrs Alberto to seek her assistance.

The ball passed again, but this time, a pair of unsteady hands dropped the catch.

The woman introduced herself curtly as Dolly, but she had a hard time speaking. Her feeble body was destroyed by years of alcohol abuse. She was grossly underweight. It seemed like she needed pebbles in her pocket to keep her from blowing away with the wind. Her words came out like staccato notes, detached and separated. She told the group she suffered from cirrhosis of the liver. Her drinking was a result of dating men who liked to drink, and who encouraged her to drink heavily. The tipping-point, however, came when she lost a baby she carried because she couldn't stop drinking. She felt suicidal after that, but ironically, turned to alcohol to drown her sorrows.

Dolly stretched out her arms and tossed me the ball.

"Can I just choose to listen today?" I asked after the catch.

I simply did not have a story to tell. I thought I was a conservative drinker. But as per Anne's test, I failed and fell in the category of an alcoholic. Instead of spending the money on fake obsessions, I chose alcohol. I berated myself for overdoing it sometimes, but I was never found lying drunk on the street or being rushed to the hospital for a failing liver or alcohol-related health issues.

"Of course you can, Danny," Mrs Alberto replied. Just then, the doorbell rang, and Mrs Alberto stood to answer it.

We waited in silence, blinking at each other. I felt overwhelmed by the stories I had heard.

The woman Mrs Alberto led into the room was a prepossessing sight. Her rich black velvet hair flowed in waves and crashed on her shoulders. Her Amazonian figure sat well on her thin body, and her glossy skin created a mesmerizing *avatar*. She had alluring and bright eyes, and I couldn't look away from them. Her pencil-thin eyebrows eased down gently as she blinked her thick, black eyelashes. Her calamine-pink lips appeared supple and kissable. Her arrival was noted by the entire room.

Her entrance caused a long silence. She chose the seat right next to me. *Oh! God, I am blessed*, cried my inner voice … or was it the only empty seat in the circle? Regardless, I continued staring.

Not content to be just another drone, she wore vibrant clothes, white with big purple and magenta flowers. I kept looking at her as though she were a beautiful apparition that could disappear at any moment.

She appeared self-centered and reserved, oblivious to her surroundings. The men stared hard; the women stared harder.

I could feel the awakening of motivation and enthusiasm.

I glanced at the tattoo she wore: a young girl with mercury red hair flowing through her uncovered body with flaming wings and the devil's horns adorning her head. I saw it as a representation of good and bad, like yin and yang.

I leaned over and whispered, "I like your angel-devil tattoo."

She lifted her head and looked at me and asked, "Are you talking to me?" as though such a thing was forbidden.

"Well, I am not entirely sure if anyone else in this room has an angel-devil tattoo," I said, enthusiastically.

"Thanks," she said, flavorlessly.

"Daniel Carvalho." I smiled, forgetting all about Mrs Alberto's deliberate choice to leave out last names for the class.

She gave a half-smile and was least interested in replying to that.

"Apologies for the late entrant. She would like to call herself Karen," Mrs Alberto said, trying to reclaim the group's attention.

There was no diamond ring signifying an engagement and no standard, cultural gold band signifying a marriage.

"Ahem." Mrs Alberto took the ball from my hand and passed it over to Karen.

"Mrs Alberto, can I just pass today?" she asked.

"Sure." Mrs Alberto passed the ball to another young lady, Ellie.

Ellie didn't look like she needed any help. A well-groomed lady, she held a notebook and pen in her hand. I thought perhaps she was doing some research work for a college magazine.

So we were all curious to hear her out. She was in AA because of her parents, she said. They couldn't contain their drinking habits, jumping in and out of sobriety. This caused a lot of tension in Ellie's mind, which made her feel suicidal. Right from the age of five, her house had been a war-zone. She hated returning home after school. She seemed very nervous while talking. Sensing the discomfort, Mrs Alberto went around Ellie's chair and placed her hand on her shoulder. An act of comfort, I guess. Ellie started to cry. We all came around her to give her the comforting group hug.

Karen remained seated.

There was silence again, but this time, faces were dark and frightened. With the end of the introductions, Mrs Alberto called it a day. She sensed we'd had as much as we could handle in one day.

Mrs Alberto requested us to cogitate on a quote by Vincent Van Gogh while holding each other's hands.

"If you hear a voice within you say, 'you cannot paint,' then by all means, paint and that voice will be silenced," she read aloud.

Karen put out her hand, permitting me to hold it. Her skin was soft, and her nails manicured with red polish. She curled her fingers around the dorsum of my hand, and a tingling sensation ran down my spine.

"We need to control the voices in our head. Our thoughts need to be challenged by us. Thoughts are merely influenced by society. Habits can be mended. To win a fight against your own inner demons is the toughest, but what you have got to understand is that if your mind has the power to create it, it has the power to reverse it," she said, ending the gathering and providing us with information on our next meeting. Wow! Those were some powerful words.

Karen rushed out, and I followed her. I watched her from behind a healthy green foliage in Mrs Alberto's garden as she got into a dark green Cielo car with tinted windows that drove off quickly, as if they were rushing to catch a flight. She never bothered to look behind.

Fingers crossed, hoping she would attend the next session, I hopped on a motorcycle taxi colloquially called 'pilots'. I had Karen on my mind all through the ride back home.

When I got closer to home, I saw Anne, sitting at the veranda, waiting impatiently for my arrival. I waved at her from a distance. She opened the gates and walked towards me. I noticed her anxious, questioning look, but I ignored it, as I walked silently with her into her house, ransacking the kitchen for some food. She sat on a short wooden stool, bouncing her leg.

She held off asking any questions, but I could tell she was having a hard time holding her tongue.

"How was it?" she finally asked when she could hold back no longer.

"Okay," I replied bluntly, stuffing my mouth with bebinca and vanilla ice cream.

"How many of you were there?" She tried to suppress her anxiousness as she kept her voice level.

"I dunno. Seven. Maybe more," I mumbled, my mouth still stuffed with the mouthwatering bebinca, a multi-layered pudding made with flour, eggs, sugar, coconut milk, and cardamom-nutmeg powder. With a dollop of vanilla ice cream, it made an impressive delicacy.

"Did you find it helpful?" She wasn't satisfied with my responses and continued her questioning.

Sensing my disinterest in the subject, she uncrossed her legs and stood up and walked out of the kitchen. I was so overwhelmed from the meeting, that I didn't see it fit to walk down that road again in my head.

John ran towards me and compassionately jumped into my arms.

"Let's play hide-and-seek," I told him.

He nodded vigorously. Often, I struggle to communicate with John, but he did a fantastic job of lip reading. Vocabulary usage was limited to 'let's go play'; 'come here'; 'good-bye'; 'thank you', and 'love you'.

I was very grateful in this moment for the distraction of him. I didn't want to talk with Anne about the meeting. I wasn't even sure how I felt about it myself. But I did know that I wanted to see Karen again.

CHAPTER 7

The Proposal

Karen's charm worked as an enchantment. I found myself eagerly waiting for the weekly meetings.

The hardest part was keeping Lawrence in the dark. I didn't want him laughing at me for going to AA, but, at the same time, I didn't want to stop going. Karen was gorgeous and I was smitten.

Anne was surprised, yet thrilled, with my enthusiasm to attend AA. While Karen was the main draw, I didn't tell Anne that.

I told her instead that Mrs Alberto had some interesting things to say.

One afternoon, she said, "Intoxication makes you lose sight of the simple pleasures. People are hesitant to reveal their addiction. Unfortunately, we live in a society that doesn't want to acknowledge their vices and would rather have them rot inside than get any help."

I suppose I knew what she meant.

I didn't want to tell Lawrence I was coming here, even if I could tell him it was for Karen. He'd tell me there were easier ways to get a girl. But once I decided on something, I didn't like being deterred.

"AA is not just about dealing with alcoholism," Mrs Alberto said. "It's about understanding the importance of life and helping each other cope with the everyday stress and bring an end to the inner self-destructive ways, and most of all, we do this together."

I liked listening to Mrs Alberto, but I still looked for Karen at every meeting.

Slowly, I got to know her, and she began to open up to me. I found out Karen was not attending AA voluntarily. She had been asked by the church and a few community members to go as an alternative to a stricter asylum.

When attendance was forced, the attendee tended to get rebellious.

She didn't have a desire to ever get sober, and why would she? She was young and was never at a loss for company. Her household subscribed to her change but never changed themselves. Both her parents were alcoholics.

Besides drinking, she regularly abused prescription drugs. I really wished I could talk her out of doing drugs. The irony was that I sold the shit she smoked.

We got too close, too soon.

Karen was intimidating initially, but once she was blissfully comfortable with her surroundings, she was impossibly lovely.

Neither one of us cared too much about AA then.

After AA meetings, we would stop at Don's Liquor Store and pick a bottle of rum and watch each other drink it away till the very last drop. She was the one woman who could match me drink for drink.

Sometimes, she carried marijuana with her.

Anne patiently watched me living in the moment, but with subtle warnings, she was trying to steer me away from Karen and her company. Female jealousy exists in every walk of life, but I hadn't thought Anne would be a part of that bandwagon. I began skipping her karaoke parties to go clubbing with Karen, Lawrence, and the group.

I remember our first kiss. I remember it because I was stone-cold sober and we were smiling so much that our teeth clanged.

In the beginning, everything felt perfect: the butterflies in my stomach, the longing for her call, spending hours together talking about nothing at all. I had been there and done that, so I knew this was a honeymoon phase, but I still wanted it to last. Last forever.

I planned on an official proposal tonight. To test the waters, since we hadn't really spoken of lifelong togetherness, I chose to swap the diamond ring for a red rose instead and utter five little words instead of four. *Would you be my girlfriend* would be apt. *Will you marry me?* That would make me more nervous than her. Would she decline the proposal? Was it too early? I really liked her, maybe even loved her. Admittedly, the odds seemed very good and in my favor. I had a good feeling about this.

I spent a whole day cleaning and deodorizing the house. I probably should've cooked dinner, but I still had no foolproof way to boil an egg. I ordered chicken *biryani* from Lucky's Biryani Hut. It came with a lot of side dishes. They specialized in Biryanis.

I set the dinner table with cutlery I picked from a local store at Panjim.

Setting the table just like they would in a four-star hotel (five might be stretching it for my place), I waited with unbridled anticipation.

It was 8.10 pm when I heard the sound of *khush, khush, khush* and then the iron gates rattled.

I shifted the curtain to the right to peep outside and saw a bright pink scooty pep enter my realm. I watched the rider take her helmet off and place it on the moped. It was Karen all right. I recognized her, even though she wore a multicoloured scarf around her nose and mouth. She also wore a thick black motorcycle jacket, and her beige shorts showed off her long tanned legs.

The sight of her set my adrenaline pumping. I opened the door before she could ring the bell.

I was surprised by the amazing vision that stood before me. She didn't look like the girl I had seen on the bike. With her jacket and scarf now in her hand, she wore a strapless sweetheart neckline, revealing her slim shoulders. A corset top flaunted her arresting torso. Her three-inch black heels made her tower over me.

She kissed my cheek and then stepped past me and walked into the house, inspecting it. I took the scarf and jacket and put it on a hanger and hung it in the cupboard.

She did not see the dinner table, yet. She walked straight into the bathroom, and I heard the gush of the water in the sink. Some form of ablution she indulged in when she stepped into a house?

I waited for her with a bottle of wine and poured her a glass when she stepped out.

"Hi," she said, wrapping her arms around me in a quick hug. I couldn't hug her back as I had the bottle and wineglass in my hand. She smelled of weed. She smoked-up before coming? Why? Was she nervous?

I lent her a glass and poured some wine and directed her to the dining table. Taking a huge gulp of her wine, she beckoned me to follow her into the bedroom instead.

She sat at the edge of the bed and loosened her high ponytail so that it fell teasingly on her bare shoulders. I watched her intently.

I had spruced up the bedroom with red sheets and green pillow covers. Quite a contrast, but I liked it.

She tapped the bed sheets next to her. I sat there.

"Too close for comfort?" she asked seductively.

"Kind of," I replied huskily, nervous of how my body responded to her thigh against mine and how she read my mind with such accuracy.

She held my chin and, lifting it, kissed me. A kiss that seemed to last an eternity.

Her tongue moved along my jawbone as though searching for something, until it brushed the delicate part of my ear. Her light breath around my earlobe made me shiver. Her nearness alone drove me to distraction. I couldn't concentrate on the proposal bit I had planned out. Although we had kissed before, tonight everything felt different.

My hands found their way to the back of her corset top, and unclipping it quickly, I tossed it aside, exposing her. Her skin was so soft; she smelt like flowers. I had never experienced such feelings before with any girl, or perhaps it was that I have never been sober enough to experience this sweet, divine pleasure. I didn't know how far I was going to get tonight, but I feared nothing. What I wanted was right here in front of me. I could hear my own heartbeat. It was thumping like a horse's hoof at the derby.

It was wonderful, amazing, this building up of sensation that grew so intense that the pleasure was terrifying.

I drew her back into my arms and settled her head on my shoulder before pulling a duvet over our bodies.

My last thought before I slept, was that she was more than just a sexual encounter. That night, I was convinced we were soul mates. I wondered how she would react if I told her I was a drug dealer. I would promise to change that if she was willing to spend the rest of her life with me.

Hugging each other as we lay in my bed the next morning, her cell phone rang. The ring startled us. "Who can it be this early?" she asked. We were still spellbound from last night, and didn't know morning had arrived.

The phone was within my reach at the bedside table. I picked it up and curiously looked at the caller ID before passing it over. Karen's unnaturally sugary voice greeted the caller, while she gestured for me not to make any noise.

"Morning." She listened and then grew agitated. "What are you talking about?

I am at Sujata's place." Her voice shook. The caller definitely had some authority and control over her life. In the few weeks that I had known her, she had never appeared so nervous.

"All right," she finally said. Karen almost dropped the phone as she took one huge breath with her mouth open.

"Is everything all right?" I asked, rubbing her back in consolation.

She jumped out of bed and into her shorts and pulled on the top that was lying over the table lamp where I had tossed it last night. Grabbing her scarf and purse, she quickly headed out.

"Hey, hey, hey." I stopped her at the door. "What's going on?" I asked in puzzlement.

"Nothing." She seemed distracted and annoyed that I was blocking her way. "Later, Daniel ... please." She glared at me until I moved, and then she opened the door, jumped on her bike, and sped out. I stood at the doorway, watching her until she disappeared from my sight.

Why did she have to rush? Who was the caller? I recalled her caller ID that read 'BOO'.

Did she mean 'boo' as in 'scary' or 'boo' as in 'partner'?

She had sounded more scared than affectionate. Surely, the former, I thought. My proposal would have to wait.

Out of the corner of my eye, I saw a little figure jumping about.

My peripheral vision had picked up a jumping jack in Anne's garden. It was John, jumping up and down and waving, trying to catch my attention. Boy could he jump! It appeared as though he were jumping on those inflatables they use at the play centers.

"Karen?" Anne said, greeting me with a nod.

"Are you spying on me?" I asked her, my gaze travelling her face.

"The unfortunate proximity," she said in a gravelly voice, glancing at me and conveniently blaming the shared garden wall of the row house.

"She is gorgeous, isn't she?" I was quite sure that Anne had scanned her from head to toe.

"She certainly is," she said, careening towards the steps and disappearing into her garden, obviously not wanting to discuss the subject any further.

John and I started dribbling the ball around. I passed the ball with a hard kick. John couldn't stop it, and the ball went rolling into Anne's garden, knocking over a few pots of roses. I hadn't told her that I stole a red rose from her garden to present to Karen. She would kill me. She loved her plants. I often caught her speaking to them. She had a different language with her plants, difficult to comprehend. She grew cherry tomatoes, curry leaves, capsicum, and a few flower-bearing plants.

She would pluck the flowers once every week and donate them to the church garland maker.

"What on earth!" she yelled at the two of us, angry at us for knocking over the flower pots. "Stay away from my garden!" she warned us.

"Sorry, Anne." I apologized.

"Just because you've been *busy* last night with … her," doesn't mean you can't be careful." Jealousy definitely laced Anne's voice.

I knew she probably didn't want to discuss Karen, but still, I couldn't help it. My head was filled with her.

"I really like the girl," I told Anne. "I really wish I could see her more."

"Be careful what you wish for," she said flatly and continued gardening.

Anne was unhappy. I wanted her to accept Karen, but she saw her as a bad influence. I knew I shouldn't care, but I did. What Anne thought mattered to me. I thought if Anne could just spend more time with Karen, she'd like her better.

So I planned on organizing a fishing trip, for Anne, John, Karen, and I to spend some time together.

*

The trip happened a couple of weeks later. Tricol boasts fresh seafood of an unbelievable variety in its deep waters. We drove through the winding road and reached the top of the hill, and then made our way down to the water. The water was deep blue and very clear; in fact, at some places where it was shallow, we could actually see the bottom.

I got my fishing gear out as Karen and Anne talked behind me. I went straight into action, with John following me. I opened a can of live worms and pierced a mass of the wriggling creatures onto the hook.

John stood there open-mouthed, unable to believe what he was seeing. It was all new to him. Anne hardly had time to take him to any outdoor activities.

I arched back, casting far out.

I turned around to watch the two ladies I had left behind.

Women somehow cross the stranger barrier faster than men. They always have things to discuss.

We put up day-camp. I carried fresh mussels as a backup. Nothing beats chilled beer with fresh mussels marinated with coconut fenny.

It was a splendid evening. I had my greatest catch of fish in a decade.

By the look of it, Anne liked Karen, too.

At Anne's house that evening, I asked her what she thought of Karen and my interest in proposing to her.

"She is a bright girl, Daniel. Although you must have gathered that I am unhappy. It is simply because I don't think you can make real progress at AA with her. She doesn't want to be sober. I blame her for the distraction. About the proposal bit, you may need to ask someone else. The subject of relationship or marriage is a little tricky for me to discuss. All I can tell you is that both require hard work. People say opposites attract the yin and yang: seemingly opposites who balance each other out. I don't believe in that. I think the differences should be kept to the minimum," she advised.

"What do you mean by that?" I asked, confused.

"For example, when I met Agnelo, he was the lead singer in a rock band. I loved how he used to hit the highest notes and was very proud of his fan following. Personally, though, I preferred soft rock to hard rock. After we got married, I hated hearing his music. It just sounded like noise to me," she explained.

"Hmmmm … I get it," I said.

"Think about it. At the end, it is entirely your decision," she said as she waved goodnight.

I mulled over Anne's advice. *What's the rush?* I thought. Karen wasn't fully aware of my occupation. I delayed the proposal.

Karen and I enjoyed our occasional rendezvous.

One night, as an assignment from AA, we were to do one good deed on New Year's Eve, as groups of three. Edgar, Karen, and myself teamed up and went with my suggestion: putting up fliers outside clubs, warning about the dangers of drinking and driving.

We decided to join the party at Club Mambos after posting the security guard to do our job by tipping him. Edgar, Karen, and I danced the night away. I chose not to drink that night in remembrance of my parents' tragedy. In fact, that night changed me. I was considering a future with Karen. I wanted to be the inspiration for her to quit drinking. I realized, too, that as much as I wanted to think I didn't have a problem, I really did.

Everything I'd learned in AA suddenly came into focus for me in that night. I had a problem with drinking, and I wanted to stop. It seemed so brilliantly simple all of a sudden.

That night, whenever Karen asked me to get her a drink, I requested the bartender to lessen the shot, lower than 30 ml.

I had just gotten her a drink from the bar and was headed towards her.

Out of the blue, a six-foot, well-built man stormed in and whisked her toward the exit door. We all ran to her rescue, only to be introduced to him as her fiancé.

The ground beneath my feet felt like it was parting ways and I was being sucked into the hollows of the earth. I watched them go, but she didn't even turn around to look at me, not once.

I called Lawrence.

I told Lawrence everything, about AA and what I really felt about Karen.

"I am sorry I hid all this," I said.

"Chill, Danny. You were trying to fix yourself, unlike the rest of us, who think we don't require fixing," he said supportively. He was as shocked as I was that Karen had a fiancé. He saw the sparks between Karen and me growing stronger every day.

"What was she thinking?" he asked, as we sat together at his house.

"She wasn't!" I said.

"She was troubled. You knew that." He patted me hard on the shoulder. "Danny Boy, don't be disheartened. You got caught up in the moment. It happens to all of us."

That night, I spent countless hours thinking about the time Karen and I spent together and wondering why she never had admitted having a fiancé. I should have read between the lines. 'Boo' calling her, and the fact that we never discussed that night at my place.

I looked for answers on my ceiling but found none. I felt heartbroken and lifeless. This world was a mere cesspool.

Karen had come into my life from nowhere, and left without even saying goodbye. I recalled a quote-discussion we had at one of our AA meetings about something Ismail Haniyeh said:

"Some *people* think that the truth can be hidden with a little cover-up and decoration. But as time goes by, what is true is revealed, and what is *fake* fades away."

"Life goes on. This is all a part of our learning curve." Anne gave me a warm hug and allayed my worry. She requested that I continue AA. I wanted to quit, but I didn't. I had made some good friends there. Edgar and Nico among them. *Orkut* was our medium of exchange, and we stayed in touch after our sessions. We had AA in our pockets through Orkut chats. Whenever we felt like a drink, when temptations were strong, we would pick up the phone and chat about going fishing or just wind each other up on silly jokes to let the moment of temptation pass away.

My life before AA was chaotic and unreliable. I had begun to realize that after my parents died; I succumbed to alcohol to shield myself from the pain I felt. I might have started out going to AA meetings thinking I didn't have a problem, but after hearing others speak and telling my own story, I began to realize I did belong there. In the beginning, it was all about Karen, but in the end, I stayed for me.

In the group, we lived off each other's little achievements in overcoming the addiction. I did not want to let them down. Nico and Edgar were the best things to have happened to me. Thanks to Anne. Nico and I would work around our geographical locations to figure out where Edgar's speech on

HGH and steroids would be beneficial. After the support group, we hit the gymnasiums and sports clubs.

One meeting day, we learned Dolly had died. We all knew she was sick. She'd skipped the last two meetings because she'd been at the hospital. She did not want any visitors. She wrote to all her loved ones from her hospital bed.

She left us a note, which Mrs Alberto read in one of our meetings:

"Life is really simple. Straighten up before it's too late. Goodbye. I tried, but I knew that as long as I lived, I would always remain powerless over alcohol."

I felt so sad hearing that. But I felt we could all learn something from her death. Sometimes, we just throw away our lives by snorting and smoking and drinking. Why not try living instead? It was that moment that I really realized I wanted to live a sober life. Not just for friends or for a girl I wanted to impress, but for *myself.*

Chapter 8

Samara

It was strange to think of the unexpected twists a man's life could take, and one morning, my life changed forever in a way I could never have imagined.

It all started with yet another early morning knock on my door. Somehow, the knock didn't feel right. My sixth sense told me something bad would happen if I got up to answer it, so I didn't.

Not that I would've, anyway. I was still hung up a bit on Karen, and I spent a lot of time in bed. She'd hoodwinked me into thinking it was real love. Dolly's death made me realize life is too precious to just give it away. My quota of emotional stress was met for the month.

I used a pillow to cover my ears, fully expecting Anne to take the message for me.

Eventually, the knocking stopped. I could hear two women in conversation, one voice was Anne's, and I couldn't recognize the other. The conversation sounded garbled.

Soon, Anne was at my window. Pushing the curtain aside, she called out in a loud whisper, "Daniel, please open the door."

"Have you lost the key?" I looked at her in bewilderment.

"I haven't. But you need to attend to this. Please open the door now!" she said again, louder this time.

I glanced at her face through the window and saw her looking as pale as a ghost, and frightened. Her expression moved me to action.

"All right, let me get my clothes on."

I nervously ran towards the door, suddenly wide awake.

At the doorstep stood a young lady; her face screamed twenty-something, yet her style of dressing classified her in the mid-thirties. She wore a fit and flair polka-dotted chiffon dress. Her raincloud grey eyes gazed at me over her puffy, heart-shaped lips.

Her jewel-laden hands carried the most angelic face I had ever seen. The baby wore a gorgeous pink crochet tutu, with a matching satin hairband, and a blooming peony on her onesie.

"Ahem." The woman cleared her throat. I glanced up at her, startled, and then back at the baby. I didn't know any babies. The woman glared at me, unimpressed. The baby cooed at me, and waved a fat fist.

"I think you've got the wrong house, miss." I ignored her disapproving stare.

"I wish it was," she replied with a sigh. "You're *Daniel Carvalho*, aren't you?"

"Well, yes."

"Then I have the right house."

She continued staring at me for a few more seconds. I was drawn to the angel she held in her arms. Normally, babies held no fascination for me, but something about this one drew me in. She looked familiar somehow.

"May I come in." It wasn't a question. It was a demand.

"I don't understand." I looked at Anne for some explanation. She refused to meet my eye and stood silently, staring at the baby. She was so still, she seemed almost like a statue. It reminded me of Lot's wife, who disregarded the angel's admonition to look back and became a pillar of salt.

"I thought she said I would be looking at a gorgeous, responsible young man. My sister always made the wrong choices," she said, shaking her head scornfully. Sister? What on earth was she referring to?

"Excuse me?" Now, I was starting to take offence. She had obviously knocked at the wrong door, and why would she think I was irresponsible just by looking at me?

"Who are you?" I asked, wondering if we might have slept together. I didn't think so.

I wouldn't date or take to bed an arrogant, off-putting woman like this one.

"I am Adelyn's sister." Her lips quivered as she spoke.

That bit of information did nothing to help me.

"Adelyn who?" I replied blankly. "I don't know an Adelyn." At least, I thought I didn't. Was she the tall brunette I met last month at that rave and dream trance house party? I didn't even remember her name, but it just came across my mind that she could have a sister who looked like the woman who had invaded my privacy.

Or was it Elsa? She kind of got all emotional over three glasses of beer because she was mid-divorce. I had a hard time getting her out of my house the next morning. I learned from *that* mistake and swore never to take a woman in the middle of a divorce to bed again.

"You don't know." The woman just stared at me, shaking her head. "Adelyn told me you might not. So she gave me this!"

The woman waved a purple stone pendant in front of me.

The pendant I *did* remember.

"Damn! Yes! Adelyn!" It all came back to me. I never really called her by her full first name. "Addie", her pet name, was used more often. Pretty girl I met in a bar a year ago. She called her necklace an amulet. Had been into all kinds of new age stuff.

"How is she?" I asked, feeling a little nostalgic. It had been a one-night stand that turned into something more—a month-long relationship, which back then was all I could handle. My favorite memory of her was the fact that she could laugh at herself. She would have some great conversation starters and made interesting points even when piss drunk.

We had a few good weeks together.

"Dead!" the bitter woman spat out.

I nearly fell over. "How? When?" I sank down in my sofa, pursuing the thoughts of the time I met with Adelyn and how she had wanted more out of the relationship. She wanted me to commit, but I didn't have it in me then. I ceased my thoughts and directed my attention to her sister, who looked fixedly at me.

"Two days ago. In a hit-and-run accident," she continued.

I found it increasingly hard to talk. I stepped aside and watched them enter my currently unkempt house.

I barely had time to process this bombshell before the woman dropped another one.

"And *this* is her daughter." She held up the baby. I blinked fast. *Daughter*?

"Hers *and* yours, Daniel." She held out the baby to me, and I just stared at the her chubby face, frozen. *Mine*? What did she mean, *mine*? What stuff is this woman smoking up? *My* daughter? My mind raced back to last year. We'd had a little fling. Had we always been careful with protection? I honestly couldn't remember. We drank a lot. We smoked a lot of pot. I … had no idea. Could this baby be mine?

I stared at the baby's face, frozen. Did she look like me?

"Can I?" Anne intervened and took the baby into her arms.

The room spun. I thought for a minute I might faint. Or throw up. Or both. How could this baby be mine? I extricated my thinking that was just springing garbage.

"No." I shook my head and sprang to my feet, pacing. "She can't be mine! Adelyn would've *told* me. I never … I never even knew she was pregnant!"

"She tried. She said you told her you weren't ready to settle down." Adelyn's sister looked like she wanted to punch me in the nose.

I recalled then, distantly, Adelyn seeming to want a more serious relationship. She'd confronted me one night, finding me out with another girl. I'd been drunk. Too drunk to deal with it. She'd been furious. It's why the relationship had ended, but she never told me she was pregnant. At least, not that I remembered.

This could not be happening. This … baby, could not be mine.

"What's the baby's name?" Anne tried to break the uncomfortable silence gathering around us.

"Samara. She is not baptized yet. You must do the responsible thing." She looked at Anne.

"Hold up!" I shouted. "I am doing nothing!" I said in sudden truculence.

"You want a paternity test done? DNA?" Her expression changed. The confidence in her tone sent a shiver down my spine.

"Yes. I would like that!" I demanded. I was not going on a roller-coaster ride with this woman. How dare she talk to me with that tone and choose to leave this baby with me? I would make that decision, not her. She seemed determined, however. I looked at Anne again, but was met with a frigid stare.

"We have a conception date report. Adelyn had that done. She wanted to get it to you. But hesitated. The love and duty for Samara, the joy of motherhood surrounded her like a halo of happiness."

"Adelyn dated *lots* of men. I mean, I wasn't the only one!"

"You think my sister is a slut! You bastard. She didn't sleep around!" The sister glared at me with vindictiveness that surprised me. "I hate to leave Samara here, but I am bound by a promise I made to Adelyn. A deathbed promise I made at the hospital that I am forced to oblige."

Deathbed promise? How binding is that? Victor had made a deathbed promise to his mother to marry her friend's daughter. He didn't keep the promise and got married to the girl he had dated since high school.

Would the dead ever know if the promise was kept or not? And why would you consider keeping the promise if it was agreed to in an extreme condition and under the influence of certain circumstances?

I didn't care what she was saying. My head was spinning.

"Don't worry, doll. I will get you out of here soon. Samara, this is your dada…" Her lips snarled with rage at that introduction.

"Why don't you attend to her, then?" I said, my suspicion growing. Why wouldn't she want Samara? Would she keep a deathbed promise even if it meant harm to a baby? Something was dicey here.

"I have two kids of my own. My husband and I barely make ends meet. I told Adelyn that I would be able to manage, but she declined the offer." There you go. She could not afford to keep her, or her husband was not for the idea.

"But I will get her out of here soon," she repeated. "I'll save up and come back for her. But for now…" She looked brokenhearted as she touched the baby's cheek, who was being warmly snuggled by Anne. "Samara, this isn't goodbye," she told the little baby, who cooed contentedly and reached out to grab her aunt's finger. She dropped two huge bags on the table, pushed a folded stroller near the door. Tears sprang to the woman's eyes. "This isn't goodbye. I'll be back. And yes, remember my name, it is Suzanne!"

She handed Anne a piece of paper that contained her contact details

She glared at me. "You take good care of her. Or I'll call child services." Then she bit her lip and spun on her heel, stalking out of the house.

"Wait! You can't leave her here! You can't!" I ran after her, but the woman jumped into her car, tears streaming down her face, and drove away. She hadn't even left a number. I wasn't even sure how to get in touch with her. How could this be?

I walked back inside and saw Anne talking softly to the baby, bouncing her in her arms.

"What did she mean by that?" I asked Anne, my voice quivering.

Anne was rocking Samara. Her arms were filled with love.

"Child services can come take her away if you're not careful."

"Why can't they just take her now? I mean, I haven't even taken care of a goldfish before."

"They can't. Not legally."

"Okay, cool. So I keep the room messy. I won't clip her nails. What else can I do to have the child services come in earlier?" I needed to pass Samara on. She was a cute baby, but I knew nothing about babies. I was the least responsible person I knew!

Anne looked disgusted with me.

"Take some responsibility. You are a father now," she said.

"Shh, Anne!" I wanted her to stop her ranting and let me think. I paced the room as Anne gently rocked the baby.

I called Lawrence and told him to get over as soon as he could. I heard fussing from the living room. "She is feeling uncomfortable. Maybe hungry," Anne said, as she read the baby's face.

Pointing to the bags, Anne asked me to check if there was anything in there for Samara.

The bag was stuffed with baby stuff. All of it. One bag had her formula milk, diapers, wet wipes, clothes, socks, and mittens. The other was filled with toys.

"Wow! How can a tiny, toothless, hairless creature require so many things?" I asked, bewildered.

"What's going on here?" Lawrence entered my open front door and gawked at the baby in Anne's arms.

"Lawrence. My Man." I felt like I needed a big brotherly hug.

"All's well?" he asked. His eyes fixed on Anne and the baby she was feeding.

"Baby number two, Anne? Couldn't even tell you were pregnant," he said, looking tenderly at the baby.

"Very funny, Lawrence. This is an addition to your family, not mine," she said sarcastically.

"Huh?" Now it was Lawrence's turn to be mystified.

"Her name is Samara." Anne held her up. "Darling, wave a hello to 'Uncle' Lawrence."

"Gosh! Cut the crap, Anne," I remarked, still feeling like I could keel over at any minute. A baby! What was I supposed to do with a baby?

The ground beneath my feet seemed to wobble.

Somehow, it still felt like some silly dream that I wouldn't dare repeat. This definitely could not be happening. Why was life giving me so many lemons? Big, sour ones!

Meanwhile, I explained to Lawrence the sudden turn of events.

"Is she framing you?" Lawrence questioned after, while walking towards Samara.

"I don't think so," Anne answered for me.

Lawrence picked up Samara and instantly turned into a warm pile of goo.

"Aw. Sweetie-pie, sugar-plum, munchkin, raspberry-dollop, chweet-heart," he cooed at the baby. I'd never seen Lawrence like this. Baby talk? That was a whole new dictionary of baby words he had just mumbled out.

Still seeming to be under some spell, Lawrence asked the most jaw-dropping question of them all, "Can I keep her?"

"Yes! Please," I said in a jiffy before he changed his mind.

"Daniel!" Anne cried, appalled. "No, Lawrence. You can't have her!" she thundered, silencing every voice in the room.

"Why, Anne? Lawrence is willing to adopt her!" I didn't want Anne to talk him out of it. I mean, here there was a man willing to care for her, and who had the money and the resources to do so.

"A baby is a huge responsibility, and the adoption system is not easy. You can't just ask for the baby and get her." Anne was trying to bring some clarity into the emotionally elevated zones we were in. "Besides, I think he was joking," she countered.

"Not really," Lawrence said. "I've always wanted to be a dad. I think I'd be a good one." Lawrence cradled the baby lovingly in his arms.

"The adoption system is hard," Anne said. "The hurdles are many, and there are some you probably can't overcome. Besides, this is Daniel's baby. He needs to take responsibility for her," she said, raising one eyebrow.

"How hard can they be?" Lawrence asked, as though nothing was tougher than selling dope.

"Firstly, a single man is not eligible to be an adoptive parent. Do you even pay your taxes?" she asked, throwing a cold look his direction.

"Hold up. Are you saying that a single woman is allowed to adopt but a single man can't? Why this disparity?" Lawrence looked offended. "And I thought love was all you needed to bring up a child." He shook his head.

"Anne," I said, interrupting the debate, "let's leave the adoption thingy. Lawrence can take care of her without the rigmarole of the adoption process."

I turned to Lawrence. "Brother, I need your help."

Lawrence put his hand on my shoulder. "Don't worry, Daniel. We will find a way," Lawrence said, trying to console me.

I rushed to my mini bar to get a drink. I stopped to touch Samara, who looked sleepy, sedated by the milk. As I was turning away, she held onto my pinky finger and said, "Da...da."

A sudden surge of emotions gripped me.

Maybe I was wrong about giving her to Lawrence. I looked at her angelic face and recognized my own eyes staring back at me. This was a little part ... of me.

Should I really give her up? I couldn't just toss her around like an unwanted ball, could I?

I knew when I looked at her soft brown eyes that all she wanted was love. How hard could that be?

I felt my heart swell in love and recognition. I looked at her sleepy eyes and took her into my arms. I gazed at her tiny face, and an all- encompassing love surrounded me. I placed several soft kisses on every inch of her face.

Anne and Lawrence were watching me, inundated with love.

"Do you still want to send her away? She is yours," Anne asked, tentative, almost fearing my answer.

"If I kept her, and that's a big ... if ... would you guys help me?" I asked.

Tears streamed down Anne's face, while Lawrence stood speechless.

"To the new addition," I said, raising Samara just like Rafiki had raised Simba on the pride rock in *The Lion King*

Chapter 9

Fatherhood

Feeding a baby is such a time-consuming exercise. Anne wanted me to observe her and then follow the drill. She fed the baby a bottle as she rocked, singing *dol mojea bai*, and then, when the baby had finished most of it, she sat her up and rubbed her back in upward strokes to move the gas up. Baby *burrrrrrrp* was now a sound of satisfaction, like a slot machine hitting a jackpot. This became a drill that had to be repeated four times a day. Not forgetting the mashed food in between. Holy crap on a cracker! Isn't there a robot that can feed babies?

"You would need help. Adelyn, by now, should have gotten Samara off the bottle." Anne said. I thought to myself, *Of course I need help. I need all the help I can get.* This was going to be one long haul. "We will stay over to help you make it through the night, and then you can take over from tomorrow," she said, assuring me of her full support.

A hint of happiness lightened my face. Anne caught that. I grinned a little too wide. I had never felt so relieved. She placed Samara in the stroller and left with John to pack for the sleepover.

I watched Samara sleeping in contentment after being fed. I looked at the parent-facing push chair stroller, sure that it had been Adelyn's choice. If only she had mentioned the baby, maybe, just maybe, we would have a different set-up today. Truthfully, I wasn't sure how I felt about Adelyn. Would I have married her? I didn't love her, and yet, part of me thought I would've tried to make it work. For Samara's sake.

But I never got the choice.

Anne returned with John. I must've looked distracted and in my own world, because she frowned.

"It's time to get serious now, Daniel," she said firmly. "Go pour you alcohol down the drain, flush the remainder of the drugs in the bathroom. It's time to gear up. You have a baby to live for."

I nodded my head feebly in response. I obeyed everything happily. I wanted to be the best dad I could be for this little one. I would take a leaf out of Anne's book. Responsibility for a baby was a major life-changing event, and then, suddenly something hit me! Responsibility! For how long? Forever? Till death do us part?

I couldn't sleep that night, waking at every little sound Samara made.

Also, I couldn't stop wondering if I'd made the right decision. Was keeping Samara truly best for her?

Sleep-deprived nights, complete abstinence from alcohol, drugs, and nights out. Could I handle this alone? On my own?

I really didn't think I could. Yet, what was the alternative? Send her to an orphanage? My thoughts battled each other. What had I gotten myself into?

Even when Samara slept, I still couldn't sleep; every little murmur she made roused me from slumber. Then, when I finally would drift off, she'd wake up with an ear-splitting cry.

It seemed I'd never get a full night's sleep again.

Nervously, I started chewing at the skin around my fingernails as I sat across the bed where Samara and John lay sleeping. The two of them wore smiles in their sleep. *I'd be smiling too if I could sleep,* I thought bitterly.

Yet, the more I looked at them, the more angelic they seemed. Sweet, even. I took a picture with my phone. The shutter sound woke Anne, who was resting on the chair next to the bed. I apologized for the disturbance and went over to show her the picture. She smiled and ruffled my hair with her hand.

I went back and sat across the bed, watching the two tiny tots. A few minutes later, I heard Anne shuffling about in the kitchen, and the smell of coffee filled the room. Anne made it just the way I like it: not too strong, with fresh milk that has been whisked to create foam, and a teaspoon of sugar.

She joined me on the floor under my quilt. The fruity freshness reminded me of the night I kissed her.

"You will be a wonderful dad, you know," she told me. "I see what a difference you have made in John's life. The football lessons, the bike rides." *Huh! How does that even qualify?* I thought. I don't hate kids. I can babysit them for thirty minutes, max, as long as they return to their home and not mine. Or maybe Anne was talking through experience. Like a defined set of rules that a man exhibited that would qualify him as a great father.

"You think so, Anne?" I turned and eyed her, wondering if she really meant what she said. She nodded.

"But I am a hustler. How can I take care of her?" Worry thronged my head.

"Quiet now. It is about taking one day at a time," she said, breaking into a song. "*One day at a time, sweet Jesus.*"

"Would you help me?" I asked, reaching out and holding her hand.

"As much as I can and more." She kept her voice low, and right then, I remembered how soft her lips were. Her eyes were so understanding, so kind. "And if you haven't noticed, it appears she sleeps well. You will get plenty of sleep. Adelyn must have been a pretty disciplined mother, where sleep was concerned." Anne wore the belief convincingly, and even I believed her.

Just then, a strange smell permeated the room. We looked at each other, wondering what the hell that smell was.

"Did you just break wind?" I asked.

Anne slapped my chest, her eyes filled with suppressed laughter. Then she went up to Samara and started sniffing her like a dog. She then indicated for me to come and join her in doing the same. I was walking toward the bed, fighting the urge of throwing up as the smell of baby poop got stronger. I clipped my nose with my fingers as Anne opened her pamper. Samara seemed undisturbed by all this.

"Get the wet wipe and a change of Pampers, please," she said, wearing a smile on her face as she watched my fingers clipping my nose.

I quickly returned with the required. "Get prepared for a poop fest, Mr Carvalho," she said, still giggling.

"Phew! Anne! I can't," I said, worried that I would definitely fail this task.

"Chill, Daniel. I will help you a couple of times, and look, it's not such a messy job. You can use hand gloves if you'd like." The smile was stuck on her face as if it were painted there. Soon enough, the horrible job was done. I had never imagined babies could be so … smelly.

Samara woke up with all the nudging, gurgled happily, and I picked her up. Soon enough she went back to sleep, without any intervention. I placed her in bed and went back to our space on the floor, in the quilt.

Soon, Anne collapsed on my shoulder and fell into a peaceful, exhausted sleep of contentment. A few strands of her hair loitered on her face; I raked through them with a delicate hand and cleared her forehead.

I watched Samara, who had a border of pillows created around her to avoid her falling off the bed. John was lying next to her, blissfully sleeping.

How tough could it be? I thought. *Take each day as it comes,* I told myself, and shut my eyes to let sleep take over.

I woke up a couple of hours later to the aroma of *bhaji-pao* prepared for breakfast. Samara and John, both were not in bed.. I looked around for them, and then I saw the splendor of love unfold before my eyes. John was feeding cereal to Samara with a tiny spoon on the floor. I stopped and stared.

Anne was laying the table for breakfast. She set out bacon, eggs, oats, and orange juice.

"Wow! What's the occasion, Anne?" I followed her to the kitchen to check if she needed help.

My once-unused kitchen was brought to life.

"I just woke up early," she replied.

I went up to Samara and John and dropped a kiss on each of their cheeks. Samara, in excitement, turned into her commando crawl position and started paddling hard as though she were trying to swim to me.

Anne read Samara's excitement. "She wants you to pick her up," she said. I picked her up, and she grinned at me, a big, gummy smile. I forgave her in that instant for losing sleep the night before. I put her in the stroller and pushed it to the dining table for her to sit amongst us.

There was a knock on the door. It was Lawrence. After greeting Samara, he wanted to get right down to business.

"So, this is how it's going to be, Daniel. I will arrange the meetings for you, and I'll try to keep them to one a day. Anne would look after Samara for that time," he said.

"Hold up!" Anne reprimanded. "You are shying away from our agreement, Daniel. You will need to follow a few steps first. You will first work on Samara's baptism. Then you will rejoin your engineering college. You have a year to go, right? I have a part-time proposition for you, where money-making is concerned. One that does not include being a drug dealer," she said, with eyes blazing like a dragon that spits fire.

"Hey!" Lawrence countered. "You can't just take my best salesman off the market. I need the man, Anne, and no part-time proposition of yours would provide him any kind of lifestyle."

All I did was turn my head left to right, hoping to form a truce by accepting both propositions.

"Do you guys want Samara gone?" Anne thundered, silencing every voice. "If the child services get even a whiff of what you do for a living, she is sure shot gone!"

"What do you mean, gone?" I questioned, bringing the argument to a halt. "She is my daughter! There is no way they can take her away from me!"

"Lawrence. Daniel. We have to act responsibly, and I am confident you would agree." Anne collected the dishes and marched off to the kitchen.

Lawrence whined. He was angry, yet treated Anne's words with great kindness and understanding. "Such a blackmailer, she is. But an awesome lady as well. You have to admire her tenacity." He turned to me. "Okay, go do your thing. Follow Anne's lead. In case I need you, I will give you a shout."

After a lengthy silence, he spoke again. "*Baba,* just one. That Cliffy Fernandes, he likes doing business with you."

"That has to change," Anne came out of nowhere and interjected.

"Fine, Miss Hitler. Your rules now!" Lawrence waved goodbye and left.

*

Samara's baptism was a private ceremony. Suzanne was invited by Anne. She came along with her two kids. The look on Suzanne's face when she approached Samara was priceless. Samara didn't seem to be attacked by a case of stranger anxiety, however, when Suzanne approached and requested me to pass her over, she clung to me like a trinket hanging tightly onto a bracelet.

Suzanne wasn't disturbed by Samara's anxiety. In fact, she was happy with the connection she saw between us.

On the church grounds, after the ceremony, we were greeted by Mrs Samantha Rodrigues.

"Oh, what a cutie. Your daughter, is it?" she asked with the timeless look of curiosity on her face.

"Yes," I replied, as I watched Samara rub her little nose with her palm.

"Who is the pretty mother?" She wanted to feed her curiosity. A lie would be inappropriate. Now that I was getting my life back on track, I would rather start by telling the truth.

I then told her of the untimely tragic accident that killed her mother, Adelyn.

Maternal empathy overcame her.

She touched Samara's plump cheeks and gave her a blessing and then walked into the church.

Anne came rushing towards me. "That was Samantha! What did she say to you?'

"Nothing much. Just asked me if she was my daughter."

"She is a nosy witch." Anne disliked Samantha for prying into the affairs and business of others. She had a history of trying to appear as if she sympathized, but then back-stabbing people, she told me. She was quick to paint a negative picture and had spread rumors over Anne's divorce.

"Oh, Anne. She is not up to anything. Samantha likes Samara."

"Yeah, yeah, yeah!"

Nosy Lady Parker, Samantha, informed the other neighbours of their new little entrant.

Neighbours began to pour in to extend best wishes and congratulate me.

Not too long after, a kind young girl in her twenties dropped a bag of baby clothes off at my house. "Mrs Braganza couldn't come in. But she sent these." Without introducing herself, she rushed out.

"She is Mrs Braganza's caretaker," Anne told me after the woman left. It reminded me of the introduction Mrs D'souza had given of her.

"All right, Daniel. Time for me to leave you and Samara to spend some time together. Call me if you need any help." Anne waved goodbye. John wanted to stay, but Anne instructed him to leave us alone.

I wanted to stop Anne from going away. But, in my head, I had promised to take care of Samara, and I had to do this on my own and in my way.

It occurred to me that I'd have to baby-proof my house. I rearranged my living room, kitchen, and bedroom, making sure nothing dangerous was on the floor for her to grab.

Thankfully, Samara was a lovely child. I had an alarm clock set for every six hours for her feed. She played with her toys on her own while I watched TV. I carried her around when she was a little restless before going to sleep.

Wow. This wasn't bad at all. Or so I thought.

Then, one night, she cried profusely. I logged onto the Internet and looked for the possible reasons but found too many to count. I called Anne.

The doorbell rang. Anne, along with Samantha, were at the door step. Anne had a frown on her face, probably because she wasn't expecting nosy Lady Parker.

"What happened?" Anne rushed to get Samara.

"I heard the wailing and rushed over," Samantha added, explaining her unexpected presence.

"I don't know," I said, handing Samara over to Anne. "She just wouldn't stop crying. I've tried feeding her, burping her, changing her, everything."

Samantha gave me this suspicious glance and came close and started taking deep breaths. She thought I did not understand what she was implying. She was sniffing me out as if I was drowning Tanqueray. I stuck to cigarettes and fizzy drinks ever since Samara stepped in. Hard for people to believe, but it was the truth.

"She's just passing gas. Colic. Are you giving her *carmicide* regularly?" Anne asked.

"Ah. No. I skipped that bit," I said apologetically.

"Make sure you close the feeding bottle tight, and don't let her suck air, and always have her sleep on the left side. It assists in digestion." Anne ran through more helpful tips. Eventually, Samara slept calmly.

"Hey, aah … you think you can stay over tonight?" I had lost sleep and was hoping for company. An idle mind is a devil's workshop.

She took a couple of seconds before she agreed. Samantha's arched eyebrows delayed her response, I guess.

"Thanks, babe. You are a blessing. I will go get John." I walked Samantha to her house and then went over for sleeping John.

"Why don't I shift in here, considering that I practically live in here more often than my own home?" she said in fun sarcasm.

"Yes, please, why don't you?" I said, hoping to cajole her into this proposition.

"Yeah, right!" She shook her head, tucked herself into a quilt and sacked up.

*

The next morning, Mr Rostiyaad stopped by. The name meant a homeless man, but it wasn't his real name. We just called him that because he spent most of his time out in the open. Samantha thought he was crazy. His girlfriend had committed suicide under mysterious circumstances. Nobody ever found out how. Many puzzled about why Mr Rostiyaad would claim he was haunted by her ghost. Samantha said he was too drunk to see a ghost; he was always hallucinating.

But then again, I thought Samantha had some pretty crazy tendencies herself. She was a friend and an enemy rolled in one.

Mr Rostiyaad came to pay a visit to Samara. He brought his guitar along and played some happy tunes. John heard the music and came over to join. So did the other neighbours.

The once-quiet house was now buzzing with activity. The little girl filled the house with so much happiness. The once-scattered neighbours were drawn to the chuckles and cries of their new resident.

I guess motherless children attract that kind of attention. Everyone's life is better with a little help from their friends and family and neighbours. Every time I would find myself in a glitch, someone would help.

With the introduction of Samara, all of us, Lawrence, Anne, and I, began moving along new paths. I re-discovered life.

I relished the idea of going back to where I had left my engineering college. Getting back on track seemed like a good proposition. But first, I had to find a way to support myself that didn't have anything to do with drugs.

One day, I carried Samara over to Anne's house.

"Hi, cupcake, my cuddle-muffin," she said and took Samara from my arms. She didn't bother to greet me, though.

"Ahem. Hi, Anne," I said.

"Oh, hi, Daniel." She turned around for a fraction of a second and then went on to talk to Samara.

"*Anne*," I interrupted. "You mentioned a proposition for me to earn some money?"

"Should we call her Sam or Sammy? I like Sam. What do you think?" she asked, completely ignoring my question.

"I like Sam, too," I replied. "Anne, I was enquiring into your proposition for me to earn some money."

Anne smiled at me. "Ah, yes. I was waiting for you to feel the need."

"What is it?"

"Well, I was thinking of wedding photography. I know Gerard, who freelances in video shooting. You could team up with him and do photography. I usually refer all my clients to Gerard. I will strike a deal with him."

"Photography?" I had no experience with photography!

"I think you would be good at it. You take a lot of pictures with your phone. You've got a good eye," she said.

"Cameras for wedding photography are too expensive, Anne. I don't have any equipment or anything!" I blubbered, before sinking into her couch. I couldn't see how this could replace my income selling drugs.

Anne placed Samara on the floor and asked John to watch over her.

She walked me into her bedroom and handed me a Cannon Digital SLR.

"Wow! You seem to have the answers for everything! Thank you! When do I start?" I asked, giving her an eager hug.

"Soon. Get in touch with Gerard. Here is his number," she said, handing me her phone book to jot the number down. I promised I would. Gerard owned a photo studio and specialized in special occasion photography and portfolio shoots. Anne used her contacts to get me the job in his studio.

*

That same week, I filled out the enrolment form of St. John's Engineering College to start where I had left off.

Life couldn't be busier.

I had to make a lot of sacrifices. Anne's contribution was immeasurable. I attended college in the mornings, and then spent the rest of the day juggling between studies and Sam and occasional photography events.

I clicked a lot of pictures of Sam. Documenting every moment. I learnt a lot of the camera settings through the countless pictures I took of her.

What a constant source of inspiration Samara was to me!

One fine day, Suzanne visited. She seemed surprised to find Samara happy, and me looking after her well.

"Seems like there is no need for the child services. You are doing a fabulous job," she said.

She went over to Sam.

"Hi, cuddly-wuddly. I miss you." Sam turned away from her aunt, busy with a new toy. Suzanne looked sad. "But you seem to have forgotten me!" She dug in her bag and pulled a small plush panda bear out of it.

"Look what I got for you."

"Panda!" Sam said and reached for it.

I was shocked by the new word, and so was Suzanne. We both looked at each other, eyes wide.

"She's got such a vocabulary!" Suzanne cooed, and I had to agree. I suddenly felt like I was going to burst with pride. Vocabulary was something I worked on with Sam regularly, thanks to Anne's "one word a day" tip. I glanced at Anne, who sat with John near the kitchen table. She nodded at me, knowing how much I had been working with Sam.

Surprised by the turn of events, Suzanne gave me a cheerful hug and left. Anne squeezed my shoulder, glad the visit had gone well. I felt grateful to Anne, as always, but in the moment, I realized I felt something else, too. As I watched her walk away from me, I realized how strong our bond had grown. I found myself slowly falling in love with her. It had nothing to do with wanting sex, and everything to do with mutual respect. That was new for me.

CHAPTER 10

College and Kylie Adams

My brief hiatus into the drug world was over. I needed to increase my chances of being employable, and I had a daughter to look after, so returning to school seemed like the best thing to do. Thankfully, Mrs Dalia, a student counselor at St. John's Engineering College, a dear friend of my mother, had put me on a sabbatical, rather than taking my name off the register, so returning wasn't as hard as I'd thought.

Entering the campus, I found a lot had changed. The notice board placement, principal's cabin, staff room.

I admit, I was a bit nervous.

"Daniel, welcome back, dear," called a familiar voice. It was Professor Raiturkar. She taught me Analog Electronics in my first and second year. She hadn't changed a bit. In her fifties, she still defied Father Time. She stood at the

113

corridor and looked at me with bottomless sadness, making me wonder whether she found me malnourished.

"You must miss them dearly," she said, after gazing at me intently. It took me a couple of seconds before I realized she was referring to the demise of my parents. I felt a rush of something, almost everything, fear, panic, sadness, grief, anger. Yes, I did miss them still. I wondered if I'd ever *not* miss them.

"Hey, Daniel," another voice came from my other side. I saw Professor Simon there. "It is so good to see you," he said, clapping me on the back. "Good decision to get back, son." He taught Digital Signal Processing. He had the same sorrowful look that Professor Raiturkar had.

This is it! I had to bring this to an end before it followed me throughout the remainder of my college year.

"Thank you. I'm doing fine," I said with my shoulders perked up and a certain confidence in my voice. I didn't want to dwell on the past. I was glad when they disappeared into the staff room, ending the spate of unwanted sympathetic glances. It made me feel as if I had buried my parents only yesterday.

The first few weeks at college were tough. I was apprehensive, literally thinking of reversing my decision.

I felt ancient in the classrooms. I was just a couple of years older than most of them, yet, I found it hard to fit in. I was a single dad. I used to sell drugs. I'd lost both my parents. I had just experienced too much to be as innocent as my classmates.

Thank God for Solitaire card games.

I had forgotten how to have the youthful kind of conversations. The girls in front of me, for example, had something cheeky to say about everyone who walked into class.

"Look at the rock star walking in!"

"Caked up."

"Panty-lines. Damn! Hasn't she heard of thongs?"

"Wow! That boy is mine."

"Could he have worn those pants any lower?"

The boy diagonally opposite was advertising some hair gel to a bunch of enthused classmates who loved his stiff Mohawk.

A forty-five-minute lecture felt like a whole day. I had the attention span of a goldfish! However interesting the subject or the professor, I couldn't concentrate beyond eight minutes.

I chalked it up to my sleep deprivation.

I took the last bench, as it gave me a holistic view of the class.

I texted Anne to find out how she was doing with the kids, hoping they weren't weighing her down. I texted her, *Snoreee…I wish I were in bed!* She replied by sending me a picture of the trio making faces. Anne squinted, while John put his tongue out with his hands on his head, and my little Sam was being fed lemon by crazy Anne. She had her lips twisted, with her shoulders raised high in reaction to the sourness. My heart filled with love. I wanted to be there with them, but I knew class was important.

I texted back, without thinking, *My lovely family! Miss you!!*

Then, I realized what I'd written. Would Anne take offense? I'd put her and John in *my lovely family*.

I waited, glancing anxiously at my phone for a reply. It came quickly.

Anne texted back: *DITTO!*

Thank God.

The class was interrupted when a college peon walked in with two *firang* students. They were introduced to us as international-exchange students from South Africa.

My mind wandered along the thoughts of 'why would foreigners want to study in India'?

Learn lots for less, I guess.

All eyes were glued on the new entrants. They were whiter than snow. The big-boned, auburn-haired girl took the vacant seat in the front row. There were quite a few vacant seats in the class, considering the first few weeks are more of an adjustment of divisions, subjects' et al. The blonde girl, who was the prettier of the two, was spoilt for choice. She had both guys and girls wanting to sit next to her. She walked to a few desks as if teasing them and then glanced around. Looking at the end of the row, her eyes met mine. I quickly dived down into my book, scribbling a poem. I paused and looked at the class ahead of me, slyly. Their eyes followed her every move.

She came and plonked her oversized bag on the desk beside me and took her seat. I shot her a quick look.

"Hi, I am Kylie Adam," she said in a thick South African accent, lending out a hand for a handshake.

"Daniel Carvalho." I held out my hand, and she shook it firmly.

Professor Simon clapped, hoping to once again gain control of a distracted class. "Class, can we please continue?" Professor glanced at Kylie. "*I* will be grading your assignments, not them! So choose who you want to give more attention to," he said on a lighter note. Professor Simon had a funny bone. Unlike the rest of the stoic professors, Simon Mendonca liked his job, and his attitude reflected it. His classrooms were always noisy, not because he didn't know how to control a class, but because he welcomed boisterous debate. It made for fun learning.

Just then, the bell rang.

"Darn the bell! Have a great day ahead!" said Professor Simon as we all stood to go.

"Daniel, want to go to the canteen?" Kylie asked and called out to her auburn-haired friend, whose name I learnt was Tina.

I love my solitude, but decided a little company wouldn't hurt. We had an hour break before our next lecture.

I nodded, accepting the invite.

Kylie took a couple of strides ahead of me and then stopped. "Which way to the canteen?" she asked me.

In the weeks that I had been present in college, I had not visited the most popular hangout, the canteen, and because of the structural changes the school had undergone, the previous canteen space was now a recreation room.

I looked around for any floor markings or overhead directions that read *canteen,* but, unfortunately, there were none.

"You haven't been to the canteen yet?" She sounded surprised.

"S-sorry," I stuttered.

"Let me have the pleasure of escorting you there," she said with a tee-hee in her voice.

It wasn't hard for her to get directions. *Pretty white girls get offered rubies quite often.*

In four minutes, we walked through a long corridor that stretched out into a large, spacious area with tables set in four long rows each. The canteen was full of chitter-chatter. I could barely hear Kylie speak, let alone comprehend her heavy South African accent.

There was a small window that served our requests. We quickly grabbed a chicken sandwich and sat down on the only available seat.

The chatting grew softer. I looked around and noticed all eyes were on us, or rather, on Kylie and Tina. Kylie seemed unperturbed by the stares and whispering, but Tina felt self-conscious with the attention.

"How's the sandwich?" I couldn't find a better thing to say to break Tina's feeling of awkwardness.

"Pretty average," Kylie chose to answer over Tina.

"Average? This is the tastiest meal we have had in two nights." Tina now grinned at a frowning Kylie. I understood they were not just classmates, but roommates as well.

"You ladies cook up your meal?" I was aware of how nonsensical our conversation was, but it helped in diverting the stares.

"I cook every night," Kylie said.

"Really? What was for dinner last night?" I asked. Her well-manicured long nails told a different tale.

"Cheese sandwich with green olives."

"Between. We do not call a cheese sandwich with green olives dinner!" I said. I was just passing some valuable information, just in case she chose to invite a Goan for dinner and would offer a cheese sandwich. He would consider that as a starter.

"What about the night before?" I asked.

"Cheese sandwich without green olives." I laughed, and so did Kylie and Tina.

"I wish people would stop staring," Tina blurted out, as she couldn't hide her irritation anymore.

"Yeah. I didn't think we'd stand out so much," Kylie seconded Tina's statement.

I didn't see their fairness as a problem, only as an advantage, but now that I saw all the unnecessary gawking at Kylie and Tina, I started to rethink my opinion.

"You have a girlfriend, don't you?" Kylie squinted up at me.

"I don't," I answered, wondering where she got that impression.

"Why would you ask?" She didn't answer. "Why, Kylie?" I asked again, dying to know the reason behind her question.

"Esmeric." She laughed.

No freaking way. She read the poem I was scribbling on my book. How could she?

"Don't worry. I just read the title. It was written in block letters; the running handwriting I could not understand," she said, grinning.

I was silent.

"Chill. Your secret is safe with Tina and me," she said, elbowing Tina to acknowledge that.

"I do not have a girlfriend. I like this lady. It's complicated, though," I said, not sure what magic this

119

newfound company had that I was pouring out my heart to them on our first meeting.

Seeing that I was comfortable discussing it, Kylie opened my book, which was lying on the table, and turned over to the last page, knowing where I had written the poem.

I tried to stop her, but after a slight tussle, I gave in. She read:

Esmeric
I find myself staring into her gaze, so mesmeric
This ineffable feeling of affection, Esmeric.
Unfettered, untrammeled love
My opium-filled days I will write off.
You made me hold on to hope
I take an oath, through all obstacles I will cope
A strong reliance, a brick wall
Lifting me up, never letting me fall
An angel's advocate
Guiding, leading, creating new life adequate....

"Very nice. Very deep. When do we get to meet her?" Kylie asked, springing to her feet to keep the serving tray on the clearing rack.

"A little too early, don't you think?" I replied.

"Nah! It's never too early, always too late," she said, pouring a glass of water from the dispenser.

While she was at that, I took notice of what she was wearing. She was dressed like a *hippie*. Wraparound bright green skirt with an even brighter, orange kurti. She had a feminine, flowery look to her that was completely misleading, because there wasn't an ounce of femininity in her personality.

She had a tattoo on her foot. A baby dragon.

"Do you like it?" she asked, catching my gaze.

"Nah! Not a fan of tattoos." I hated conversations on tattoos. Reminded me of Karen and her angel-devil tattoo.

She went on to tell us how painful it was to get inked on the foot. She had one under her arm as well, a sailor's compass. Likes them where it hurts the most, that one.

"What about you, Tina? Followed suit?" I asked.

"Tattoos? Why on earth would I convert a momentary pang into pain? Have a permanent tattoo over a temporary body? Tattoo your soul, if anything, with kindness and compassion," she said in response.

"It's a personal choice, honey," Kylie retaliated.

"True. Pain has many dimensions, you know," I intervened, not wanting to lead this into a debate, showing them my fastrack hand watch and the fact that it was almost time to head to class.

I fell in love with my new friends. They made great conversations.

The rest of the day rushed by. Our last lecture was cancelled. Professor Kalekar was ill.

Stepping out of the classroom, I called Anne. She had the kids at the park.

While at the bus stop, I saw a bearded man taking huge steps towards me. His ubiquitous influence was felt by the students passing by.

"Oh, Boy! Oh, Boy! Daniel!" he said out loud, giving me an overly tight bear hug. How does such a powerful voice and a bear-like hug emerge from an emaciated frame like his? I pondered.

I must have looked confused, because he asked, "You don't recognize me, do you?"

I tried hard to recollect. Damn! The beard! I couldn't seem to recognize the face behind it.

"It's James," he said, cutting short the guessing game.

"What!" I remembered James. He was in my batch. Mr Richie Rich we would call him. His father owned a road construction company. "What's up with the beard, James?"

"Helps in staying anonymous," he said with a grin.

"What are you doing here?" I was happy to see him and curious to know what he was doing around the college, when he should have graduated by now.

Was it a girl?

"I cannot seem to clear the fourth year, dude."

"Whaaaat?" I shrieked. He should have graduated two years ago.

James was born with a silver spoon in his mouth. He didn't need the degree, as he would eventually take on his father's road construction business. He was just passing time.

"Serious, man," he said with no trace of unhappiness in his voice. "Chill, dude. Let's meet up whenever you are free for a game of ball," he said and left, while I waited for a bus.

*

I got on an inter-village bus and decided to go see my grandmother. It was only fair that I visit her, considering I was so close to her house. I could make a few visits every week.

The same familiar smell of the village, of red mud roads, permeated the air. I remember my grandmother would tell me not to get red mud on my clothes, as it was very difficult to wash out. I missed how my grandmother and I used to have long talks while we sat on the porch benches.

The smells that came from my grandmother's kitchen would make a full stomach hungry again.

She was talking to her neighbours from across the iron gate. She started crying the minute she saw me. She always cried when my parents and I visited and cried when we left. The bonding cry kept her healthy, my father would tell me.

"I thought you would never come to see your old grandmother," she said, continuing her crying.

"Oh! Nana. You know I would." Yet, I sounded unconvincing, even to myself.

"Come, come. You must be hungry." I followed her into her ever-welcoming kitchen. She served me sorak curry, with brown rice and fried promfret stuffed with rechad masala. I had missed her cooking.

Suddenly, I heard a dog barking from the backyard. "You have a dog!" I was astonished. Grandma hated dogs. She was always telling us how she got bitten by a dog on her behind when she was ten years old and had to go through the bitter ordeal of injections on the stomach.

"Yes. What to do? The humans in my life were either taken away from me or walked away from me." She was referring to my parents' sudden death and me leaving her. I felt a pang of guilt.

"I have gone back to college, Nana," I said, changing the mood. She cried to that as well.

"I am so happy for you, *put mojo,*" she said lovingly.

At this moment I wanted to tell her about her granddaughter. After all, grandparents play a huge role in parenting. I wasn't entirely sure if the timing was right. Despite her trendy appearance, she still retains her ancient mentality. High on superstitions and relates to a society that has zero tolerance to the irregular.

She would definitely freak; worse, hold me captive.

Nana sensed an underlying tension and asked, "Is everything all right? How are you surviving? Not into drugs or anything, no?"

Why was she asking? Did she hear I'd sold them? That I'd gone to AA? Was it just a substantiated guess?

Drug addiction has always remained a threat of great proportion amongst the youth of Goa. We have a lot of runaways returning from the black hole after experiencing life's lessons.

Anyway, I had left that world behind me. It wouldn't be lying if I said "no."

"No, Nana," I denied firmly, meeting her eyes and assuring her there was truth in my answer.

"Then what is it? Money?"

"Nothing really. Nervous about college." Now that was one big white lie. I didn't want to disturb the feeling by telling her about Sam. It could wait. She was basking in the glory of her prodigal grandson. So let it be.

"Don't worry. You have always been a good student. Pray to God; ask your parents for help. They are closer to God. They will definitely hear your plea." She routed her attention toward the two-foot altar that had a statue of Mother Mary and Jesus. My phone started to buzz. It was a text from Anne. "Home now. Sorpotel for lunch." I had already eaten, but I couldn't decline an invite for Pork Sorpotel.

After a wordless while, I kissed Nana on her forehead and promised to come by more often.

CHAPTER 11

Nursery Time

Sam outgrew her pram so quickly. She was growing up so fast. Months passed, and in the blink of an eye, suddenly she was ready for nursery school.

I managed to get a place at Bumble Bee Day Care Nursery. Dr Brenda down the road made the suggestion, and the admissions process was easier than I thought it would be. Dr Brenda, a primary care pediatrician, attended to the kids of BB; I remembered Mrs D'souza mentioning this. She took into account my current financial situation and provided not only an admission but a twenty percent discount in fees.

Thank God, for small mercies, or else I would have to stand in the wee hours of the morning in the longest of queues to seek admission and sacrifice on my engineering project preparation costs.

It was almost time. She would start in three weeks. But I dreaded it! I hated that inevitable feeling of nervousness and anxiety. I felt as if I were preparing to throw helpless prey into a predator's den.

Even as an adult, it took me weeks to settle my equilibrium in my second innings in college. How much more difficult was it going to be for Sam? Very!

I didn't believe myself. Part of me was waiting for this day to dawn. I couldn't wait for more "me" time, and yet I also worried about dropping her off with complete strangers.

Anne did mention there could be separation anxiety. Somehow, I was sure Samara would pass this phase with distinction. She never seemed to suffer from separation anxiety and the like. I guess because she had a lot of visitors, thanks to the pampering of her Uncle Lawrence, Aunt Anne, and not forgetting the neighbours.

"And moreover, separation anxiety is a behavior that kids learn from their parents. Parents have to be flexible with their babies. The more unwilling they are to part with them, the more likely the baby will have separation anxiety," Anne said in a mild voice, trying to calm my nerves. John was playing peek-a-boo with Sam.

"Anne, why don't we consider homeschooling?" I exclaimed suddenly. The idea had just sprung up inside my mind, watching the two play together. "You could teach her! What do you think?" I was excited. I even thought of collecting a few kids from the neighbourhood. Anne was amazing with kids. She was amazing with everything, actually.

"I can't," she said, glancing briefly at John and then meeting my eye.

Damn! How selfish could I be? How were we to help John with his sign language program and essential guides to navigating through this confusing world?

Anne had gotten John to take an extended leave from school to help Sam and me adapt into our new lifestyles and here I was, less concerned with how John would fit into our superficial nursery.

John had to go back to school, and he needed Anne full-time. Although Anne offered to stay on a little longer, I didn't think it was right.

So I tried my best to be confident with Sam about her first day of nursery school. I launched a 'Nursery Time is Fun Time' campaign a few days before she was due to start. I showed her *Barney* shows, where the kids get together and dance and play while Barney instructs them. I told her she was going to make many friends and play with many toys. Then I asked John to describe his experiences at his school. He drew her a picture of a classroom with kids sitting in circles and the teacher standing amongst them. He helped her understand that the teacher substitutes for a parent in the school.

"When do I get to see this place, Dada?" she asked. This question made me feel victorious.

"Soon, honey," I replied, bubbles of joy bursting in my heart.

"Early to bed, Samara," I yelled from across the living room a few days later. "It is your first day of school tomorrow; your new friends are waiting to see you. We need to wake up early or else they will go home," I said, trying to employ Sprechgesang in my vocals to sound excited.

"Okay, Dada. I am super-duper excited," Samara replied gleefully. I watched her. She had grown so much, so fast. Her tresses of silky black hair were short enough, exposing her pixie-like nose and jawbone. Her deep-set chocolate-brown eyes looked at me like a puppy dog.

"Me too, darling. I am excited for you. Get into bed now." She didn't bother replying, as she was too distracted putting Rachel, her doll, to bed.

Dolls are a girl's best friend. Rachel, a fifteen-inch doll with a plastic head, had long auburn-red brushable hair, green eyes, freckles on her face, and dimples. Samara's love for Rachel and pretend play provided a whole lot of entertainment on some evenings.

I found I had trouble sleeping, but I was up at sunrise, right at five thirty. The thought of waving goodbye to Sam every morning and wondering what she was doing at the nursery for four to five hours made my chest heavy.

The excitement of packing Samara's bag and brunch made me skip my morning coffee and head to get her Hello Kitty-themed school supplies from the attic, which her Aunt Suzanne had presented to her the week before.

I had looked over the Internet two days earlier to find ideas to make her interesting snacks, considering there were so many restrictions over what can and cannot be carried to the nursery.

I had been preparing for this for over a week now. Anne showed me short-cuts.

Slicing the thick edges off the sandwich bread, I applied a mix of the ground chicken spread that had been prepared last night.

I got my bag of cookie cutters in various shapes and sizes and picked bunny and little fishes for today's treat. I gave the bunny its face and the fish its eye with Cadbury Gems chocolate. *Phew!* One sandwich and I had managed to mess up the entire kitchen.

When Samara woke up, she was a little disoriented. Initially, I thought this was a cause for concern, but eventually, I just settled on the fact that maybe she hadn't slept well. I got her dressed while she was in her disoriented state.

She was soon ready. She looked at herself in her white T-shirt and white shorts. Spinning in a pirouette, Samara asked, "Dada, we going … play?" I just smiled. Did she not remember? Anyway, reality would hit her soon—or rather, hit us both soon.

What do I do with her hair? Her silky straight hair were never clipped or strangled into a braid or bun. But I had bought some hair clips just for today. Quickly, I pinned them into her hair. They didn't look half bad.

Stepping outside, Samara walked toward Mrs Braganza.

"Aantaa … don't cry?" Samara asked. Looking eagerly at our neighbour, she saw Mrs Braganza's head bowed down in adoration as she prayed to the holy cross figurine made of cement.

An 82-year-old devout Christian, she got fresh flowers and venerated the cross at the by-lane, every morning. This time, Samara's curiosity got the better of her. Mrs Braganza replied to Samara with a verse from the Bible, trying to break it down in as much babyish language as possible. "If anyone would come after me, he must deny himself and take up his cross daily and follow me." Samara smiled. While we were walking towards the parked car, Samara started giggling.

"What, Samara?" I wanted to know what she found hilarious.

"Dada, Mrs Braganza has gone mad. How can anyone carry that cross?" She continued giggling.

Samara always managed to surprise me with her understanding of the life around her. She meant how could Mrs Braganza carry a cemented cross that has been on the by-lane for so long. We both chuckled.

I was not sure if she was aware of the fact it was her first school day, yet.

We reached our destination. In a confused state, Samara started investigating her surroundings. We could hear wailing of children at a distance from where we were parked. I saw children clinging onto their parents' legs, some pulling garments, running in the opposite direction of the nursery, parents crying along with their children. It was chaotic; Samara had tears streaming down her face, as she begged me not to leave her. I promised I would stay—a lie, because the nursery staff whisked her off and pointed me to the door, assuring me this was all normal.

On my way out, I felt lonely. My thoughts raced as I wondered whether Samara had settled down. Was she still crying? I needed something to do to distract me from my sadness. Tears rolled down my face.

I hoped she understood. The pressure for me to leave was intense. Samara was stronger than that. I had made sure Rachel was in her bag. Some familiarity in uncharted territory. It wouldn't take her too long to recuperate. I knew my girl. I knew Samara.

Most nurseries had an introductory first-day class of two hours only. Five minutes to go. Eager and searching eyes were looking at the gates as though their staring at it would mysteriously open them. The doors finally did open, and everyone scurried in to search for the class, and most certainly inspect the reaction of their child.

"Samara, your daddy," the teacher called out. *Deceitful Father*, Samara gave me that look while picking up her bag and walking out.

The silent treatment was what I got on our way back home. Why was silence so freaking loud?

"What did you learn in school today?" I asked.

"Twinkle twinkle traffic light," she sang. *"Round the corner shining bright.*

Red says stop, green says go, yellow says go really slow"

Thank God. We need to learn the act of forgiveness from our children. So willingly do they forgive, without any hesitation, without a doubt in their hearts.

I did not see the clip on her hair.

"Honey, what happened to your butterfly clip?"

"Oh, Daddy, it flew away," she said, grinning.

She continued singing. Samara knew the lyrics to more than ten nursery rhymes. I used nursery rhymes as a bed-time lullaby. The best time to learn something is just before dozing off, and this exercise had helped Samara retain most of the songs and rhymes.

The first day of school was hard, but the next two were even harder.

I tried to be positive. Also, the feedback I got from her teacher, Ms Shabana, made me feel very proud of Sam.

"Samara is superb. At her music class, she needs to hear the song twice, that's all. She remembers the song and tune thereon," she reported.

On our way back home, I picked up the sound track of the Disney Movie *The Lion King*, which was a massive hit amongst the kids. She watched the movie, like, a zillion times over.

She loved all the songs. She knew the lyrics to all of them by rote.

She displayed beautiful intonation without even a hint of shrillness, sounding like she was eager to be king.

I bought her the book *Goldilocks and the Three Bears*, which the teacher read to them in school. I would read it to her as well.

I tried everything after school to keep her interested. I bunked college for a couple of days until she settled into her nursery.

I made sure I reached her nursery at least twenty minutes early. Luckily, my college was just a short walk away.

I mingled with some of the other parents.

"They are too small to go to day-care, if you ask me," said a well-suited parent. She probably had no choice.

"Oh! She hasn't settled in yet," said another.

It was reassuring to know that mine was not the only one. But as it turned out, starting on the fourth day, she loved school. She mentioned Anuska, her first friend in class. She couldn't pronounce her name and would call her "nuka." She had nicknamed quite a few by now.

"Nuka has a pet cat, Dada. I want one, too," she said.

"Really, Samara, would you bathe the cat and clean the litter if I got you one?" I was considering a pet, although I would prefer a dog. The bond that was usually formed between a child and the pet as they grow up was often said to be a huge factor in a child's emotional development. My parents had a dog, but they gave it away soon after I was born. They wanted to give me undivided attention, they told me. Bruno, the dog, was given to our neighbours. He didn't survive more than a month. My father told me that the separation killed him. They felt really bad after that, and continued to be dog lovers thereafter. All their lives, they supported some dog pounds in the area.

"Dada, I give bath, and I feed cat and you clean the niiitter and cut nails, just like how we have a teacher to teach, a nanny who changes our pampers, and a nurse to cut our nails," said my smart little girl. I rolled on the floor with laughter. Sam had a funny bone. She was a natural. I was sure she would make strong friendships and be well-liked by everybody.

Yet, even in that moment, I could see her moving from babyhood to childhood, and it was bittersweet.

CHAPTER 12

Despicable Me

I became resigned to the monotony of my current status quo. I went from patchy photo assignments to college, and then off to pick up Sam from the nursery. Even college settled into a boring routine. Kylie had gone back home on an emergency to attend to her ailing father, so I found myself bored out of my skull.

I was grieving over the transformation of my existence: the loss of my identity and the killing monotony of being fastened to a little one all day. It was getting difficult. There was no adult stimulation of any sort.

I had no *me* time. I only had work, study, and fatherhood.

On a beach, beneath a clear blue sky, I sat sipping on *Kings* beer and watching people go by … Of course, I knew from my brief time in AA that beer probably wasn't a good idea for me. Yet, I still longed for these simple pleasures. I envied all the students around me: no responsibilities other than class or odd jobs. The uneventful everyday chores of nappy changing, bottle-feeding, pureed food feeding, entertaining *et al* seemed endless. Babies were a routine.

I checked on Sam, sleeping peacefully in her bed, and was grateful for her, and yet at the same time, wondered who I now was.

Just then, my phone rang. I ran to grab it quickly, lest it wake Sam.

"Where the hell are you?" a voice on the other end was half-saying and half-yelling, even before I could say hello. I looked at the caller ID to confirm who it was, as the voice was unrecognizable.

"Nico! What happened to your voice?" I asked in a blaring whisper. To me, it sounded like Nico had a dreadfully sore throat.

"Got a frog stuck in it," he said, struggling to talk, yet incorporating humor. "Forget all that. What have you been up to?" he asked. I guess he was calling me to find out the reason for my absence from AA.

"You don't want to know!" I said quickly in response.

"We miss you at AA, man. Is it because of Karen?" he enquired.

Karen! I couldn't believe he said that. I didn't dwell on a mistake for too long. Luckily, I had this gift to push negativity out of my mind faster that P.T Usha's fastest 400-metre hurdles in 55.42 seconds. Or maybe a little more. But yes, fast enough.

"No way! I don't have the time to think about her. Good riddance to bad rubbish, I tell ya," I said, laughing out loud.

"Yeah, true. She was some riddle wrapped up in an enigma better left unresolved." He endorsed my opinion. "Let's meet for tea, *yaar*. I am so bored," he continued. He was actually echoing my sentiment. It would be nice to have some guy time after so long.

"You want to come over?" I asked. Stepping out of the house meant asking Anne for a favor to look after Sam. I was burdened by all the favors she had been doing for me, and I thought it was about time people were introduced to Sam as my daughter.

I awaited his arrival that evening. We'd had some nice times together at AA. The two of us always had something interesting to share. We were like two peas in a pod.

Sam woke up. I was feeding her when the doorbell rang. Every time she heard the sound of the bell, she gets so excited. Lately, it brought visitors primarily for Sam, and along with it, a bag of goodies.

"Dude," he said the minute I opened the door. He looked different. The eminent glow on his face made him unknowable. He had transformed. He looked handsome, with a full-grown beard, blue jeans, and white T-shirt.

"What's up?" I said with a tight embrace. "Nico, look at you! I would pass you by and not recognize you!" I stood back and checked him out, top to bottom.

"Huh! Not recognize me?! Thanks for letting me know. I will never have you as witness in case I am in trouble! How can you forget the way I look?" Sarcasm laced his voice.

"Hieeee, hieeee, hieeee!" Sam greeted Nico … The chuckling of a baby caught his attention. He pushed me aside and searched for the baby who carried that chuckle.

"What the—! Who is this doll?" he said, walking towards the high chair Sam was seated in with food all over her face.

"Carrieee!" she squeaked.

"Oh, sure!" he took her off the chair and looked at me quizzically, while Sam rummaged through his beard with gooey hands. I offered him a face towel to clean the mess.

"The reason I had to stop attending AA and brought my whole life to a complete halt. Meet Samara. Samara Carvalho, my daughter," I introduced her quickly and waited patiently for Nico's reaction. He stopped everything he was doing, his face a multitudinous array of complex emotions.

"Man, what stuff you smoking?" he asked with mocking laughter. He thought I was pulling a fast one on this.

"It is the truth," I said, looking him straight in the eye, so he would be able to discover the truth in what I was telling him.

He whistled, looking extremely surprised.

"I'll be a monkey's uncle! I knew you were up to something, but this was the last thing on my mind. Your young, carefree ass wouldn't know how to handle this!" he said, almost assertively, placing Sam amongst a pile of toys on the floor.

He placed his backpack carefully on the dining table and sat himself down. He pulled out a bottle of Absolute Vodka from the bag.

I was taken aback at the sight of alcohol in the hands of a member of AA who had been on the road to achieving sobriety.

"Why, if I may ask?" I questioned in a voice a few decibels louder that my normal tone.

"Why do you look surprised, Daniel? A friend was travelling, picked it up at duty free for me, and moreover, it looks like you need it more than I do," he said, detecting the signs of boredom on my face.

"Come on. One drink won't hurt no one." He helped himself to the glasses lying on the dinner table. Poured 60 ml vodka into two glasses, then raised them up and gave me one.

"No, Nico. I've got Sam and ..." I declined the glass. I'd promised Anne I wouldn't drink. And I had to look after Sam.

"Come on, Daniel. *One* drink! It won't hurt anything," Nico pleaded. "Come on, I just ... need someone to talk to. Please. One drink."

I hesitated. One drink might not hurt. *One drink would be okay,* I thought. I'd just have *one,* then stop there. Nico could talk to me about whatever was bothering him, and I could still watch Sam.

We drank the shot down. Something was going on with Nico, and if he felt comfortable talking after a few drinks, so be it. I would drink responsibly and find out what was behind this changed avatar.

It was a girl. It had to be. What was with them lately? At one point, a woman was the reason a man would change his evil ways and adorn the path of righteousness full of love, peace, and happiness, but nowadays they tend to join us in our evil path.

So Nico went on to describe his one-month affair.

One drink led to another, and soon I was drunk. I thought I could control it, but now I realized I couldn't. Of course I couldn't! I was an alcoholic. I'd be naïve to think I could just have one drink and stop. All of a sudden, I heard screaming and yelling from outside. "Sweetheart, stay there," I could hear Mrs D'souza yelling from across the road.

"Anne! Sam is on the road," she called out to Anne frantically.

Sam? Did I hear Sam? I looked around the house, calling out to her. She wasn't anywhere in the room. Goddammit! The door. It was left open when Nico walked in. Sam managed to walkout and onto the road. She was heading to Anne's place on her own.

I ran out. My intoxication drained away.

Anne gathered Sam in her arms, while Mrs D'souza was crossing the road. A few bystanders came around. Anne looked at me, puzzled.

"I can explain," I told them. With the smell of alcohol radiating not just from my breath but off my body, Anne just marched towards her house.

"Anne, listen. Don't walk away." I quickened my steps to match hers.

"You promised, Daniel! You promised!" she said, clearly vexed with me.

"Can we talk?" I stopped her by holding her elbow with a slight nudge, and tears found their way down my cheeks.

"Just go away, Daniel. You've done enough." She darted off to her house, followed by Mrs D'souza, who gave me a detestable look as she passed.

Still sobbing, I walked to the cemented cross, made the sign of the cross, after ages. I begged for forgiveness. A vehicle could have run Sam over if not for Mrs D'souza's timely intervention. "This is the most irresponsible thing any human being could be capable of," I heard Mrs D'souza say out loud through Anne's window wanting it to reach my ears.

"I think I was wrong. You will never change. I am calling child services and Suzanne," Anne said, screaming at me from across the road.

"Anne, I am sorry," I said, but it fell on deaf ears. "It was one mistake!"

Nico left, judging the scene. I went back home and puked the alcohol out and drank two liters of water, then had a quick shower to get rid of any traces of alcohol.

Bad news travelled faster than light, while good news travels at the pace of a slug. Within minutes, the whole of St. Anthony's colony was over at Anne's place.

I walked through the open door of her house, and voices suddenly silenced in my presence.

"Here he comes, shamelessly," screeched Samantha.

"I don't think she deserves to be in his care," she continued.

I ignored her outrageous comments. I looked at Anne. Her eyes were swollen from crying.

Brian Noronha walked up to me and requested that I have a seat. "Daniel, we have a suggestion. We understand you are young and have youthful desires, and a child in your life is a constraint. Instead of the child services getting involved or Sam going to live with her Aunt Suzanne, who is far away, why don't we work on an adoption agreement for Joyce and me to look after her? This way she will be around the colony, and you get to see her regularly, but we will take care of her."

If he would have come forward the day Sam walked into my life and surprised me, I probably would have fallen for that offer, but not now! Yes, I felt exhausted with the regular chores, but she was my daughter. I loved her. I didn't want anyone else to raise her.

"Look at how he dresses her up! Like *Wreck it Ralph!* Joyce will definitely do a better job," Samantha harped, with her penniless advice.

"No!" I said, with stupid never-ending tears flowing down my cheeks … again.

"Anne. One mistake and you want Sam taken away from me?" I looked at her for sympathy.

She was outnumbered; she couldn't make a biased decision. A few colony miscreants were already spreading false rumors about us.

With tear-filled eyes, I could barely see clearly. Just then, both John and Sam ran toward me and gave me a tight, compassionate hug. John, in sign language, was scolding Anne, thinking that she had made me cry. Sam, my precious daughter, was holding onto one leg so tight, and looking up at me, smiling.

I realized what I had done; my negligence could have cost her … her life!

Anne began crying profusely. I went over to her with both the kids in my arms. I placed them on Anne's lap and gave her a hug. She didn't stop crying.

The gathered saw the sparks of love and strength between us. They silently left the house.

I grew up that day. From a boy to a man.

I vowed to be better, and this time, I was.

CHAPTER 13

Eureka Moment

Reciprocation is the *prima facie* of any relationship, and a fair exchange was what held us together.

Samara enjoyed the time she spent with John. They threw the ball, played catch, and ran races, but as her language skills took off, she soon discovered John didn't talk the way she did. John used sign language to communicate, but as Samara knew none, he'd often simply have to point.

Samara, often just tell him to *talk.* She frequently asked, "Why doesn't John talk to me?"

I tried to tell her about John's limitations, but, she was too little to understand.

Anne, the mediator and translator between Samara and John, would have to spare time from her busy schedule to ensure a healthy relationship between the voice and the voiceless.

"John doesn't listen," Samara complained one day, stomping in after going over to John and Anne's house.

"Let me see if I can help," I said, moved by her frustration.

I called out to John. He had followed Samara and was eavesdropping behind the door.

"How was school today?" I asked, mixing actions with words.

He used sign language to explain it to me. With that pantomime, I gathered he had sports day in school, where he ran in the hundred-metre race. His classmate tripped him, and he bruised his knee.

Samara did not understand anything but reacted when she saw his wounded knee.

"Boo boo!" she yelled. "Aunty Anne, John got boo boo!" She went running to inform Anne.

When Samara got back home, I decided to help her with her communication with John.

"Baby," I said, "why don't you learn to talk with your fingers?"

"Talk with my fingers?" She laughed. "You mean like John, Daddy?" she asked. "Ms Shabana teaches us finger counting. I can count up to ten with my fingers, Daddy. Listen to this: One little, two little, three little fingers." She began signing with her fingers, and then went on to her toes, until she finished with the ten little fingers and toes. "Daddy, can I have two of those candies?" she asked, gesturing with her index finger and middle fingers together. She had become proficient in the skill of dactylonomy. Why not enhance it and add finger talking, too? It was just a fleeting thought.

Enrolling Samara in a sign language program seemed like a wise thing to do. This way, she would learn something new and be able to communicate with John, bridging the communication gap. A Google search did not help, as most of the classes were beyond the boundary line drawn in my head; the others were beyond my means.

There were two major forms of sign language used universally: British Sign Language (BSL) and American Sign Language (ASL). Since John was already learning ASL, I started researching it. The alphabet signing looked easy to emulate, the tougher bit was to convey the tone, since sign language conveys both context and acoustics. I wanted to leave Samara with just the basics of this physical language, to push-start the engine and allow her to manoeuvre and change the gears as she chose. I was reminded of the guessing game, dumb charades.

Done with the alphabet, the next task was to learn the vocabulary, or words for everyday use. That seemed easy-peasy lemon-squeazy as well.

I introduced Samara to twenty-one easy words to start. I was proud of her retention capacity, compared to others her age. It took us one afternoon of two hours to learn the words.

I have heard from the elders that the first five years are fundamental in a child's life. They learn more quickly during these years than at any other time in life. I needed to harness and sharpen Samara's IQ and EQ.

Excitement crept in, and we decided to surprise both Anne and John at the karaoke party she was holding that evening for the neighbourhood.

For Anne, John's diagnosis of speech disorder at the age of eleven months had been a life-changing event. I had my fingers crossed that this would bring her some joy.

That evening, Samara barged into Anne's house as soon at the doorbell was answered, and without her usual greeting, she looked around for John. Running toward him, she began with what we had rehearsed that afternoon. She gestured "I love you" in the non-conventional ASL way of pointing to herself, then crossing her hands across her chest and then pointing at John.

"Let's go play," she said, with her thumb and pinkie finger of both hands sticking out, while the rest of the fingers were tucked in, giving them a twist back and forth. Samara's impassioned act stirred up emotions in everyone. I felt my chest tighten. It was a sweet scene. "I love you, too," John replied, using Samara's non-conventional gesturing, but he ended it with another gesture we didn't understand. The thumb of his right hand went under his jaw, and then he brought the hand down on top of his left hand, with the thumb and index finger of both hands sticking out in the opposite direction like a cowboy shooting with two guns with crossed hands.

"Sister," Anne stated, reading our confused expression. "I love you, Sister," she said again.

All of us were overwhelmed with happiness at the interaction between the two little beings, trying their level best to overcome their barrier of communication, and not giving up on each other. I had forgotten what happiness felt like, my once-waddling footsteps now seemed to meander happily around the room. My daughter made me proud; she didn't fake her understanding of life, and most importantly, she wanted to impart happiness.

The next day, Samara returned from school, ate her lunch at a rate of knots, and made a dish-dash to introduce her new dexterity with fingers to her favourite obliging local.

Anne called out for a drive to Baskin Robbins, as it was one of her whimsical craving days, where she treated us to ice cream.

We were talking about the new wedding assignment she had received from a friend in Dubai, Sheina, who, besides the tailoring of the wedding gown and entourage outfits, wanted her to look into photography, video shooting, transportation vehicles, and the wedding car, along with its décor.

I could hear giggling in the backseat of the car. Turning around, I watched Samara and John gesturing in sign language, inventing their own words and signs; they were oblivious to our presence.

At the ice cream parlour, we made a list in accordance to the budget provided by Sheina of the companies and people we knew who would get us a hefty discount so that we could make some commission on it.

The discussion came to a standstill as soon as the banana royal sundae was served. Coincidentally, we ordered the same flavour, and we relished every bite, feeling relaxed, watching the passersby enjoy their various treats and ice creams.

John started nudging me and drawing my attention to a well-dressed gentleman at the cashier's counter. He was using his hands to talk to the cashier, and John understood that he was requesting extra spoons and tissues, but the visual way of communicating was intimidating, and the cashier was unable to comprehend him. John persuaded me to be the voice and convey the request to the cashier. I did just that.

On our way back home, pondering the disability of the gentleman at the counter and John in the backseat, I decided to work towards making communication easier for people with hearing and speech disabilities.

The cognitive faculty of my mind was in overdrive when, suddenly, I had my Eureka moment. "Yes!" I said, my hands clenched in a very tight fist.

"What?" Anne asked.

"I am going to create a prototype wherein I can incorporate sensors along with some programs into a glove and make it convey words through a speaker," I replied gleefully as I drove.

"What glove? Convey words to whom and why?" Anne asked. Her face had a somewhat quizzical, discourteous smirk.

"You see, general people have to learn sign language to speak with dumb people. Why not make the process easier by making the mute person talk to everybody through sign language, which is then converted into words and emitted out of a speaker?" I was trying to explain the process, but unfortunately, it looked like Anne wasn't getting it. She looked deep in thought, though.

"Why? Learning sign language is fun. I see a lot of use for it. Let's say we are across the room and need to communicate, instead of shouting out loud or digging for your mobile to message, I would throw you a gesture. Human language developed through gestures; Socrates says: 'If we hadn't a voice or a tongue, and wanted to express things to one another, wouldn't we try to make signs by moving our hands, head, and the rest of our body, just as dumb people do at present?'" She was speaking out loud. "Why do we always need a gadget for everything? Our hands work just fine!"

God! Anne! So Neanderthal in her thinking. She is one of those species who sees no good in technological advancements. She still sends greeting cards for Christmas and New Year's instead of an e-card.

"Oh, never mind, Anne. Einstein's thoughts, too, were regarded as insane," I remarked.

She started biting her tongue, trying to hold back the laughter at the comparison.

"You will see," I assured her, convinced that I would convert the idea to a product.

We reached home, and sitting at my study table, my mind filled with a plethora of ideas for the final-year project submission, I started work on the schematics of the gesture-recognition glove.

We had to submit both a group and an individual project, and I would use the glove as an individual submission. I was convinced nothing could beat this idea.

I wanted to share the idea of the glove with someone, discuss the prototype, and get feedback. I was contemplating calling Leslie, my classmate, but a bitter, distant memory made me drop the idea.

For our first term, Leslie needed programming advice and requested a meeting at Café Coffee Day. To my surprise, he made me sign a three-page non-disclosure agreement that stated that, if breached, there would be a court hearing, and he would sue me for damages. I was offended, as an NDA basically says, "I don't trust you," and surely enough, it did cripple the relationship I had with Leslie. I thought it was a sign of amateurism and lack of trust.

"Curiosity is the lust of the mind," Thomas Hobbes once said. I was curious, and it led me to sign the NDA and work out the programs for the blind spot detection, using ultrasonic sensors embedded on the side-view mirror that warn if any vehicle is in your blind spot. This mainly was to assist the absent-minded who forget to look at their blind spots.

This project gave him first place, and the idea was submitted to GE, who donated three lakh rupees to our college to set up an in-house incubator that would facilitate new idea generation and lateral thinking.

Leslie was hailed the campus hero, and he never once mentioned the assistance he got from me. Anyway, I put this all behind me and grew wiser and more innovative in my thinking.

I am not sure why I'm thinking about Leslie. My idea of the glove is unbeatable. The winning individual project would receive $100,000 in scholarship funding and a temporary job position in the research laboratory of a renowned firm in the U.S.

From being the second best in the mid-term project, I want the first place in the final term.

I wanted this for Samara. I was eager to be a hero in my daughter's eyes, eager to encourage her futuristic thinking, eager for her to understand competition, participation, and winning. I wanted to give her everything in the world.

My love for electronics manifested itself in the large cluster of circuits and tools in the spare room; it was there where I had learned to find solace.

Jotting down the ideas for the gesture-recognition glove, I snapped my head up to the unfamiliar sound of silence. *Where is Samara?*

"Samara, are you in the bathroom?" I shouted out, to which I got no response.

Rushing toward the veranda, I called out to her again. I had just gotten myself out of grave repercussion, and now I had left the door open again, and she probably sneaked out.

"She's in Mrs Braganza's backyard," Anne yelled back.

This disappearing act of Samara's needed to be curbed. That girl was a free spirit, and she just didn't think before she acted. I vowed to give her a stern talking to, as I rushed over to Mrs Braganza's.

Once there, I saw that Samara was teaching Mrs Braganza, whose stuttering had increased over the years, to communicate in sign language. Introducing a few finger gestures to both Mrs Braganza and her caretaker, Samara wanted to ease the tension between the two. She often would hear the caretaker scream at Mrs Braganza for want of clarity.

Three other neighbours joined in and were learning sign language to communicate both with John and Mrs Braganza. "*Dev Borem Korun,*" Dr. Brenda said, kissing Samara's forehead.

Turning to me, she added, "*Patrao,* your girl is a gem." I returned the compliment with a soft grin. I felt supremely proud of Samara, and I was struggling to hold back my tears.

"Daddy!" My little girl ran to me, beaming.

"Baby, please inform me the next time you decide to step out of the house," I said with my hands clenched at my sides.

Samara leaned over to give me an apologetic hug, and I felt my resolve melting. I couldn't stay mad at her for very long.

CHAPTER 14

◆◆◆◆◆

Finding a four-leaf clover

At class the next day, one of the project groups discussed an idea for heliostat solar cooking. It was Leslie's idea for the team project, and this time, he was wilfully talking about it without the element of an NDA.

"Does the world need solar cookers? Why don't we eat sushi instead?" asked Kylie, in a tone a notch above a soft whisper. She had returned from her emergency leave, and along with her, her humour. Leslie uttered a string of barely audible insults, which fell on deaf ears because the rest of the attendees were laughing loudly.

"Hi, Daniel. I was considering a project on aquaponics for the individual submission. You know about it, right? The aquaculture combined with hydroponics. I sat up last night to put the dynamics on paper. I would need some fruit-bearing plants. Any idea where I can get them from?"

Kylie shared her individual project idea with me. That was rare. Most of the classmates kept the ideas for themselves until the final day.

"Wow! I like the idea, Kylie," I said, feeling happy for her and glad that she trusted me.

"I know! I just had my landlord complaining that he did not have a sizeable amount of land to cultivate. He envied the neighbours. The idea sprang up then. I told him I will show him how to grow vegetables on his rooftop all year round." That was a great idea. This would release stress from people whose sole income depended on the agricultural output.

What attracted me to Kylie was her openness and her carefree attitude toward life. Unlike Leslie, who slyly worked on his projects and only used people whenever he thought it could help him, Kylie was open to discussion and considered teamwork and brainstorming together an advantage that added value and widened the scope for new idea generation.

"There is a village next to *Panjim City,* called *Verem.* I know a horticulturist there. Not sure if he has the plants you require, but I am sure he could suggest alternatives," I replied.

"Can we go there before class tomorrow?" Kylie was eager to start work on her project.

"Sure thing. Can we meet an hour early? I want to introduce you to my submission." *She is the right person to talk to about the gesture glove.*

"Oh, you cheapskate. You spoke nothing of the idea, and it seems like you have a prototype ready already," she said, throwing a light punch on my stomach.

I winked at that.

At our morning coffee, I shared my idea with Kylie. We discussed which program to install, and we chose a few basic words to write coding on.

The target was to change the sign language into spoken words. The objectives of this project were: learning the sign language alphabet, altering the sign language into electronic signals, converting electronic signals to spoken words, and programming the device. Kylie volunteered to help me stitch the flex sensors onto the gloves.

We helped each other finish our submissions. For our group submission, we worked on the already-existing idea of the *roti* maker.

*

Graduation time came quickly. The principal invited Father Augustus to the stage to deliver the commencement speech for the graduating class.

Father Augustus was a man of great wisdom and sagacity, a man with dominance, both of words and great acts. He acted as a counselor to the spiritually broken, emotionally broken, heartbroken, and those from broken homes.

My closest experience with him, the revelation of his benevolent side, was when he gave refuge to Roger, a teenage boy whose drinking and smoking pot had left him comatose on the street every day. Roger, now a sacristan, is a devoted follower of Jesus and a social worker to the downtrodden.

Father Augustus opened a thick book, just like our Digital Signal Processing. The only difference was that the DSP book cover page was colourful, while this was just black.

"Don't let anyone look down on you because you are young, but set an example for the believers in speech, in life, in love, in faith, and in purity—1 Timothy 4:12," he began.

"This bible verse in the book of Timothy reminds me of the Chamber Brothers' album, *Love, Peace, and Happiness.* It is these three virtues we must aim to achieve; for if we are at peace within ourselves, we learn to love, and thus, even in simple pleasures do we find happiness. We are the owners of our minds, and we need to direct them. Always have a goal and work towards it. Living without a goal is like going down a path without a destination. Education is just Chinese Democracy, if not implemented and shared with the real world. What challenges lie ahead, we cannot predict. What we can do is choose to think positively, which will help us take control of our lives and the situation at hand. Lastly, don't forget to stop and smell the flowers! Spend time with your loved ones, spend time with nature! *Dev Borem Korum, Deus te abençoe.*"

My mind drifted to memories of my past life, the Pandora's Box long closed. I am grateful to the four prominent figures whose steadfast love and loyalty kept me going, who changed this abbreviated piece of nothing into a confident young man. Lawrence for finding me, Anne, who stayed by my side through rain and storms, Samara, who gave my life a purpose, and John, who, without a voice, speaks words of strength and love.

My chain of thought was broken by a loud noise. The microphone was making a high-pitched screeching sound. Mr Kalekar, our vertically challenged professor of analogue electronics, grabbed the microphone and tapped it. The audio in-charge changed the position of the speaker so that the output of the speaker wasn't feeding directly into the mic. The irony of the situation was that Mr Kalekar taught analogue electronics... *This is exactly what Father Augustus was talking about: Education is Chinese Democracy if...*

The organisers of the event scampered on stage, arranging a changeover for the award ceremony. Certificates and trophies were placed on a rectangular table adorned with rich red velvet linen. A red carpet runner on the stairs created an aura of a *filmfare* award ceremony.

"Right foot forward," a whisper in the crowd distracted me. It was Ramesh, Project C's group leader, the smartest in class and an electronics engineer, yet no amount of education would free him from the fetters of superstition.

The award ceremony began. We were lined up to walk on stage, one by one, to receive our degrees from Father Augustus. This was accomplished in forty-five minutes, leaving behind two of the most prestigious awards given for the best idea generation across teams and across individuals.

Shortlisted projects competed for this acclaimed trophy. I was fortunate to be short-listed in both categories, but what I was really hoping to win was the individual trophy and the scholarship that went with it. Mr Kalekar began with the group winners.

"The award for the best group project goes to—" Mr Kalekar stopped abruptly. I had a flip-flop feeling in my chest, but some students had their fingers crossed, and some were chanting the Lord's name. "Solar Cooker team," he finally announced. Project C team was ecstatic with this announcement. Kylie and I looked at each other and giggled, remembering our lame sushi joke. I guess the programming used in their solar cooker was innovative. The heartbeat that had slowed down with this announcement started gaining momentum again. "Second place goes to the *roti* maker team," he announced, waving his palm, calling us on stage.

I cannot recall how exactly I felt deep inside while walking toward the consolation prize, when our group created the most innovative idea there was. Anyway, I still hoped to defeat my adversary in the individual project submission.

Snickering, as she was walking up the stage with me, Kylie said, "It's all about the food, isn't it?"

"Eh?" I said in response.

"First place, solar cooker. Second place, roti maker," she continued, giggling anew.

I couldn't hold back my laughter.

"And now, the announcement for the best project in the individual project submission category that will receive USD 100,000 in scholarship funding and a temporary job position in the research laboratory of a renowned firm in the U.S.," the principal said.

There were three good projects in the running, and it could be any one of us, but winning this was important! It would provide me with funding for my further education and a job that would help support and improve the standard of living for Samara. My daughter was the central focus of my life, and she needed this.

"The prize for the best project in the individual category goes to the most innovative idea, and has also moved the emotional quotient of the judging panel members for its noble thought. The winner is the … Gesture Recognition Glove," announced the principal. Everything stood still for a moment. My knees felt so weak with excitement that even though I was already on stage for winning second place in the group project, I couldn't take the five steps to the podium, where the principal was waiting with the cheque and certificate! *This is the moment of truth, Daniel. This is it.* My inner voice was helping calm my nerves.

With a handshake and a short hug from the principal, I received my reward. I was overcome with jubilation when I heard the clapping. Surrounded by the thunderous applause, my emotions got the better of me. *I wish my clan was here to witness this, I wish … Oh Gosh*! I suddenly realized I was going to be late for Samara's last day at the Bumble Bee Day Care. She had been preparing a skit for over a month and wanted me to watch it. I glanced at my watch. There was half an hour left for her school gathering to end. I sneaked out of the back door of the auditorium, and I made a run for it. The ceremony was still on. I sent Kylie a quick text to keep me posted on the remainder of the event.

Luckily the school was around ten minute's brisk walking distance from my college.

The auditorium was vast and silent. I looked around for an empty seat and walked straight toward it and seated myself.

Samara and John were on stage. "This is my brother, John," she introduced him to the audience.

"Together, we are going to perform 'You can count on me' by Bruno Mars in American Sign Language," she announced.

There was pin-drop silence in the crowd. John and Samara were performing with such great flair. I looked for audience reactions, and saw there were tears streaming down their faces.

How magically they moved their little fingers and hands in unison! They were applying sign language to the song. Anne had done a fabulous job of training them. My eyes were scanning the auditorium to get a glimpse of the director who brought about a crowd of tears.

I caught a glimpse of her, and she was looking straight at me. I blew her a flying kiss. She caught it in the air and trapped it in her T-shirt pocket.

A degree, a scholarship, and a job opportunity in the US—but somehow, it all felt curiously hollow.

At that moment, all the fear and tension I had in my heart was lifted. For some reason, that was the most loved I had felt in years. I was truly happy.

I felt an alarming sense of liberation.

Anne spoke to me with her presence. With her desire to get me out of my drug world and help me to become a responsible father, she had succeeded where others failed. My one companion in life. A harmonious relationship.

No one believed that the relationship between Anne and I could be platonic, and it kept the whole neighbourhood guessing and gossiping. I loved Anne, but it's the kind of love that no one writes about. It was simple—I respected her. It was her heart that I loved. Her enchanting ways encouraged me and suppressed all angst. She had this Midas touch that could bring any raging storm to sudden calmness. Her way with kids—look at Samara, a vocabulary of more than

3,500 English words at her age, the Portuguese language lessons. Samara could run for a listing in the top twenty child prodigies of India. John's disability did not bring her down; she introduced him to skating as an alternative to express himself.

Now that I was going to America, I realized that the one person I couldn't bear to leave behind, was Anne.

"You have found a four-leaf clover," Lawrence once told me. I did not understand him at the time. I looked up the meaning of four-leaf clovers. Each leaf stands for something: Love, Hope, Faith, and Good Luck.

Now I finally understood what he meant.

I need Anne by my side, to take me through life's toughest journeys. With her, I will not stumble, I will not falter. A woman who has always believed in my dreams and made reaching my goals that much better because she helped me get there.

Anne's cold fingertips on my shoulder jolted me back to reality. "Daddy, we won!" Samara was showing off her certificate of achievement for the best actress in the role play.

"We won?" I questioned.

"Yes, Daddy! Aunty Anne and John won along with me." She was basking in the glory of her victory, but not forgetting the ones who got her there.

"Congratulations, team!" I said hurriedly, my thoughts still jumbled. "Let's get to your car, Anne. The crowd will make it difficult to exit, creating a jam in the parking lot." Feeling claustrophobic and sick, I began pushing my way out of the crowd. My head felt like it was being pierced from the inside by thousands of tiny needles.

In the car, without a spoken word, John and Samara continued to communicate in silence. Anne figured there was something blocking the flow of my words, while I had my eyes squarely on the road.

A churning sea of excitement and grateful feelings were smouldering deep inside me, and I did not know how to put them in words.

Anne passed me a bottle of water. I sipped all of it in quick gulps, experiencing immediate relief. I then tossed over the brown envelope received from the ceremony into her lap. It had the congratulatory note in it, along with an itinerary of my travel details and course structure.

Her facial expressions were of extreme happiness and euphoria. Then, quite unexpectedly, she let out a shrill joyous scream. I jammed the brakes, bringing the vehicle to a screeching halt, much to the displeasure of the automobiles behind us. One driver came out and gave me a telling. I apologized, aware that I could have created a domino-effect collision.

I checked to make sure that everyone in the car was safe—John and Samara luckily had their seat belts on—and then, turning toward Anne, I asked, "Have you gone out of your mind?"

"Something like that." She grinned. The moment was too poignant to be amusing.

"Man, you surely are good at masquerading your feelings! What a sad-loser face you put up. Almost made me believe you didn't win in both fields," she said hysterically. "We need to celebrate." She reached out to her phone to dial Mrs D'souza. "Hey, guess what? He won, he won, he won!

Yea!" Joyfulness hit her like lightning. "Samara and John did a fantastic job, too. What a day, Mrs D'souza! Let's celebrate tonight," she said.

"Yes, to the U.S.," she replied to Mrs D'souza's question, which drew my attention to read through the nuances, the subtle changes in her expression, which I had learned to interpret over the last year. I can differentiate between levels of her happiness, too.

In less than four seconds, there was a vast array of emotions ranging from happiness to sadness in her voice and on her face. She cut the call and looked out of the car.

The time felt right; the feeling appeared mutual. It seemed I had always loved Anne. I pulled out a piece of paper, where I had written a poem trying to describe what I felt for her. I wrote this while in one of the boring lectures of Mr Kalekar. I handed it over to her.

"Oh, another surprise?" she exclaimed, opening the folded paper in a jiffy.

I feel stronger, yet weaker at the same time
When I dream of you, the words just rhyme
I feel at peace with the world and myself
Colorful, kaleidoscopic dreams abound

Unbridled love, uncanny touch and immense warmth
Without you, days just pass by in a trance
When you are around, there is a twinkle in my eye
Such illusory charm, it feels like a disguise

The luster in your eyes, the glow on your cheek
Every morning is so perfect, every day of the week
You make me believe in unrequited love, in its truest form
Walk through the door right now, let's embrace the storm

What is it about you, which makes me so nubile
Eyes, lips, grace, elegance, and class
Above all, we are meant to be
Because of what you do to me.
I love you.

Minus the major butterflies in my stomach, I was ready. "Anne, you have been my dopamine all along. I would want to make this trip with you. You are my backbone, and I don't want to miss having you to depend on … would you?" Finally, the words came out.

That bloody silence, after you ask the question and wait for an answer, felt deadly.

"Sim, Eu adoraria," she replied in Portuguese. A tad bit shy of the presence around us.

"Yes, I would love to," her pupil in the backseat translated.

She stretched across to place her parfait lips on my chapped-out-of-nervousness ones, and then returned to her seat, holding on to my hand, her fingers entwined in mine.

There were muted coughs and giggles from the backseat.

My family, I thought. *We could do anything together.*

About the Author

Starlette Carvalho, a professional banker, wife, and mother, always loved to write. She kept journals, wrote freelance articles for a suburban newspaper, and loves nothing better than to spend every ounce of her free time writing short stories. Carvalho, a Goan from Mumbai, earned a business degree from India and is currently working as a banker in the United Arab Emirates. Anytime she sees a blank page or a blank screen, she loves to fill it up with words.

For years, she struggled with the question of whether or not to pursue a writing career, choosing to share her work only with family and friends. Eventually, she decided this was the story she wanted to write. "It really resonated with me," she said. "I felt this story of a father taking care of his daughter and the entire neighbourhood helping to raise her just felt like something I needed to write. I grew up in Mumbai, and I think the feeling of community there is strong."

This is Carvalho's first novel.